# FIREWATCHER

## Secrets, Strategies & WWII Pineapples

***Brian D. Ratty***

Sunset Lake Publishing LLC
89637 Lakeside Ct.
Warrenton, OR 97146
503.717.1125
bdratty@Dutchclarke.com


First Edition published in October, 2022
ISBN: 9798352072691
(Sunset Lake Publishing LLC)
Printed in the USA

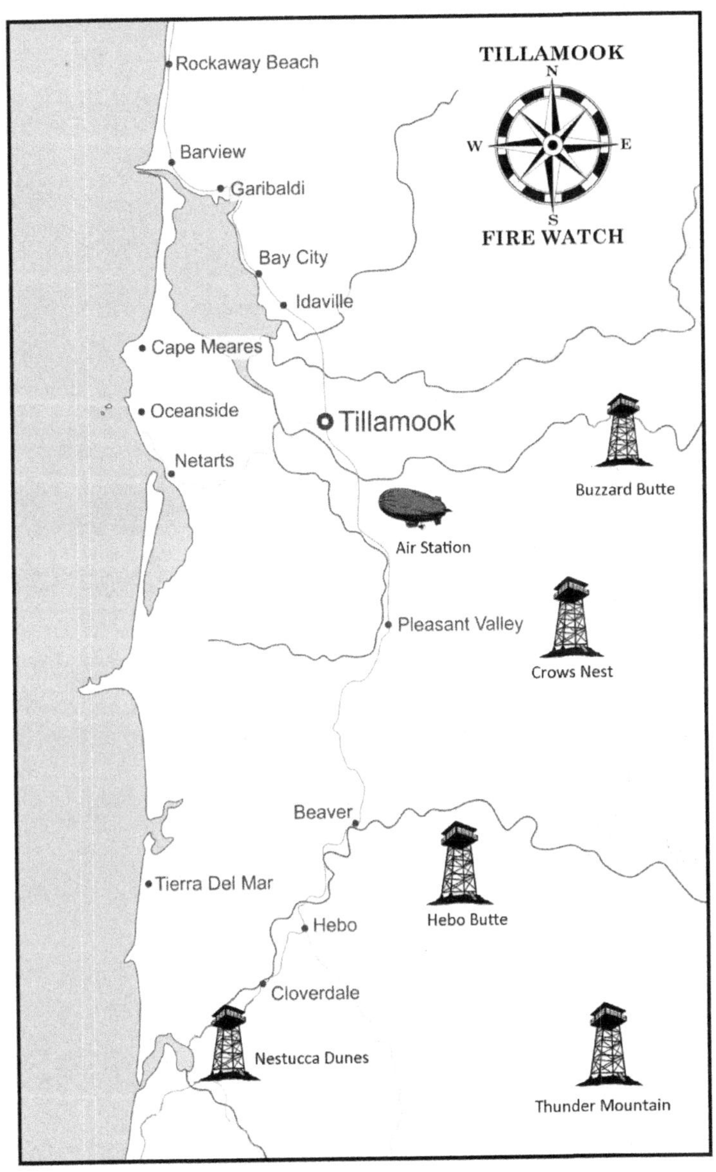
TILLAMOOK
N
W
E
S
FIRE WATCH
Rockaway Beach
Barview
Garibaldi
Bay City
Idaville
Cape Meares
Oceanside
Tillamook
Netarts
Buzzard Butte
Air Station
Pleasant Valley
Crows Nest
Beaver
Tierra Del Mar
Hebo
Hebo Butte
Cloverdale
Nestucca Dunes
Thunder Mountain

## Authors Notes

Oddities of local history have always captured my imagination. There is something special about a story that isn't absolute history *or* absolute fiction. **Firewatcher** is just such a tale, concerned as it is with overcoming the past, confronting the future, and defying all expectations. Set against the opening days of WWII, the plot concerns a young girl coming of age and learning to work with others for the common good of saving the local forest. Why the Tillamook Forest and the watchtowers of that date and place? Because timber was a protected war commodity critically needed to win WWII. Therefore, the government developed policies and protections to insure a steady flow of wood and wood products throughout the war.

**Background**

When pioneers started settling the West in the last half of the Nineteenth Century, they were confronted by vast stands of green forestlands as far as they could see. Millions of acres of trees were free for the taking without any consideration of the Indigenous population. And take it they did, with little or no thought for conservation or forest management. In 1891, the Federal Government stepped forward with the Forest Reserve Act. This act allowed the creation of forest reserves, much to the chagrin of the timber barons, mine owners and railroad companies who felt the timberlands were theirs and theirs alone. In 1905, the Bureau of Forestry became the US Forest Service, a federal agency that was then in charge of sixty million acres of timberland. With this much reserve land, it was not uncommon for lighting strikes to start forest fires during the summer fire seasons. Some homesteaders and local Indian tribes even used forest fires intentionally to clear the land and make it more productive for hunting and farming.

Then came the summer of 1910, hot and dry! In August, numerous small wildfires in Idaho joined together to create what is known today as the ***Big Blowup***.

That wildfire burned over the course of two days on the weekend of August 20–21, after strong winds caused numerous smaller fires to combine into a firestorm of unprecedented size. It killed eighty-seven people (mostly firefighters), destroyed numerous man-made structures (including several entire towns), and burned more than three million acres of forest with an estimated billion dollars worth of timber. It is believed to be the largest, although not the deadliest, forest fire in US history. The burned area was about the size of the state of Connecticut.

In the aftermath of the ***Big Blowup***, the US Forest Service received considerable recognition for its firefighting efforts, including doubling its budget from Congress. The outcome was to highlight firefighters as public heroes while raising public awareness of national nature conservation. That fire is often considered to have been a significant impetus in the development of early wildfire prevention and suppression strategies.

The Great Fire of 1910 cemented and shaped the US Forest Service, which at the time was a newly established department on the verge of cancellation, facing opposition from mining and railroad interests. In the wake of that bad year, the Forest Service adopted a policy of strict fire suppression. In each national forest, a fire detection system was organized, consisting of lookouts and guard stations. Early communications between these stations was quite primitive, including heliographs, flags and even carrier pigeons.

In 1918, women started staffing some of the lookouts. Many were schoolteachers or college students on summer break. Such a job being held by a woman alone was shocking to some, at the time.

The 1930's were a boom decade for fire lookout construction. Some lookouts were built on private timberland by the National Park Service, while others were built by the Forest Service. During the Great Depression, the CCC (Civilian Conservation Corps) helped build hundreds if not thousands of fire towers in the national forest.

***The Tillamook Burn*** was a catastrophic series of large forest fires in the northern Oregon Coast Range mountains, fifty miles west of Portland. It began in 1933 and struck at six-year intervals through 1951, burning a combined total of 355,000 acres (554 square miles).

During WWII, five hundred observation towers were staffed in Oregon. Many of these sites were also occupied by the Aircraft Warning Services (AWS) during the war.

In 1990, the Forest Fire Lookout Association, was founded. The Forest Fire Lookout Association is a nonprofit organization dedicated to the worldwide research and restoration of forest fire lookout stations. *ffla.org*

Today, a number of the fire lookouts in Oregon are still in working order and are manned during fire season. Once the fire season comes to an end, the lookouts become available to the public for overnight stays. There are twenty such lookouts in Oregon alone.

The job of Firewatcher appealed to people from all walks of life – from writers to hermits to teachers – but it was not for everyone. The solitude was attractive to some but felt isolating to others. In addition, living on a mountaintop was a rustic experience, with no plumbing, no electricity, and a hike required to reach the nearest water source. The secret to living successfully in these fire lookouts was to believe in yourself and to believe that anything was possible.

**This book is dedicated to the brave men and women firewatchers who manned the lookout towers during WWII.**

# Contents

**Firewatcher Chapter Lineup** (Part A)

**Firewatcher Chapter Lineup** (Part B)

# Prologue

**Dark Days of 1942**

Singapore falls to the Japanese
Battle of the Coral Sea begins
Japanese air raid on Dutch Harbor Alaska
Japanese submarine I-25 shells Fort Stevens
Incendiary bombs dropped on the Oregon coast
U.S.S. Astoria sunk in the Battle of Savo Island
Corregidor surrenders to the Japanese
16 million Americans will serve during WWII

Did the Japanese have a secret weapon? It was rumored they had underwater Aircraft Carriers!

# Prologue

## 1942 Gloom & Doom on the Home Front

Due to the war, sales of trucks and cars are banned
The War Labor Board orders equal pay for women
Rationing books are issued
Mostly women go to work in the shipyards
Legions of men march off to war
A new car cost $920.00 (If you can find one)
Average rent is $35.00 per month
Gasoline 15 c a gallon
Eggs 20 c per dozen
Bread 9 c per loaf
Tuition to Harvard: $420 per year

**America's Secret Weapon: The women at work!**

# Chapter One

## Daydreams

You could hear it before you could see it. The noise was unusual and indiscernible. It wasn't the early morning spring sounds of the countryside just waking up. No, it didn't sound like a manmade clang of a motorcar or birds chirping in the breeze or the wind rustling the grass. It wasn't animal, vegetable or mineral, just a strange 'clicking' sound that got louder as time rolled on. But what was that sound …and where did it come from? Then a silhouette appeared in the sunrise, moving over the crown of a hill, riding a bicycle. As the rider came closer the source of the confounded noise was revealed: ordinary paper playing cards, clicking on the wire spokes of the bike wheels. "Click, click, click" the tires yelled out as a boy's Schwinn bicycle, with a girl at the handlebars, moving down the county road with a rooster tail of dust following in her path.

It was early, 7AM early, on a beautiful spring morning of May 1942. The world had been at war for just six months and the bicycle the girl pedaled had once belonged to her older brother Nick. He was gone now! He had enlisted into the United States Marines Corps on his eighteenth birthday, just a few weeks before. The girl missed her brother desperately; they were more than just siblings they were virtuous souls. Now she enjoyed riding his bike as if he was patiently waiting for her back at the family farm. Why had the Japs taken her brother away? She hated them and all the misery they had brought the world.

The girl in the sunrise looked more like a boy with baggy overalls, a red wool shirt and a straw hat tied under her chin. On her feet were old black high-top tennis shoes with her pant legs rolled up because the bicycle was without its chain guard. Above the front wheel there was a large wire basket secured to the handlebars. On this morning, the basket contained six dozen eggs in gray paper cartons. While on the rear wheel there were wooden-clothespins holding ordinary playing cards to the bike frame, causing the unfamiliar sounds of the spokes turning.

The girl had a pretty sun-drenched face with blue eyes, blond hair and rosy cheeks from a world with the dew still on it. Beneath her baggy garb was a girl rapidly becoming a young woman, her parents had named her Ruth Ann Nelson, while her friends just called her Ruthie. She was just fifteen years old, but fibbed to those, *not* in the know, that she was seventeen years old. Ruthie was on a fast track of growing up.

Using her brakes, she pulled off the road and stopped her bike in front of the old Cloverdale School house. There were just seven classrooms inside the entire building which held students from the first grade to the twelfth. Cloverdale, with its remote location, was truly a country school.

Looking back down the road she yelled out to her dog. "Come on Winnie, you're holding up my parade. You can ride in the basket after we deliver the eggs."

She watched her dog closely as he did his best to catch up with her. He was just a pug faced mutt, only two hands tall, with stubby legs and a short brown coat of fur. She loved her mongrel and watched out for him, just like her brother Nick had watched out for her. But things were changing fast in her life and she wasn't sure how to cope with the unknown.

As she waited for her dog, she glanced at the school house. She would graduate from Cloverdale in just a few days. Completing high school in three years, not four: just like she had skipped the 5$^{th}$ grade in elementary school. Ruth was book smart with a head full of curiosity and a mind hungry for more. But her parents were poor, so there was no mention about higher education. She and Nick would be the first in the family to complete a high-school education. That achievement alone was reason for a celebration.

In the shadows of the school house, Ruth removed her hat and pumped some well water into a tin plate she had in the basket and allowed her dog to drink. When he finished Ruth gave him a piece of beef jerky, "Two more miles to Hebo, than you can ride all the way to town with me. It's going to be a long day, but you won't have to run all the way."

Winnie had walked onto the family farm three years before. He just showed up one morning hungry, whimpering and sad. He was just a stray mutt with no place to go and no one to care. So Nick and Ruth had promised their mother Helen that they would watch out for him and they had. The kids loved the little pug and named him

Winnie because he reminded them of Winston Churchill. He had bravery, curiosity and determination just like the British Prime Minister. Winnie was loyal to the kids and feared no animal on the farm. The only person he coward away from was their father, Oscar. He hated dogs, and loved to kick the mutt when he was drunk, which was unfortunately often. Their father had a dark-side which frightened everyone who lived under his roof.

Finishing his jerky Winnie looked up at Ruth wagging his stubby tail and let out a bark. He was ready to go.

Putting her hat back on, she walked her bike to the shoulder of the road and paused for a moment in the morning sunshine. Under all that tomboy garb was a pretty girl with an innocent freckled face and wistful eyes that looked as if she had a secret dream for a better life and a better place.

It was a half mile back down the county road to the 20-acre family farm that she called Shangri-La, and two and a half miles further north to the little hamlet of Hebo. She had traveled this way many times before: on foot, in a car and by bike. It was a scenic route that filled her young eyes with spectacular landscapes. She remounted her bike without another word and the pair continued their journey.

On one side of the county road there was a thick majestic forest of tall Douglas fir trees, and alders, with a sprinkling of a few red cedars. This was timber country, where forest lands were plentiful and lumber was cheap. Anyhow, that was the way it was before the war. Now with the shortage of able-bodied men to work the fields or the woods, no one knew for sure what to expect.

Across the road the view was quite different, with rolling hills of green grass, with creeks and streams for miles around. This little valley was filled with small family farms and cultivated crops of potatoes, corn, hay, barley and much more. Cloverdale was a bread-basket where during the Great Depression the locals had scratched out a meager living. Now what? Food shortages, scrap metal drives, the scantiness of gasoline, paper, sugar and coffee. The newspapers said the Great Depression was over, but was it?

**Look Back**

The Nelson's were Norwegian Immigrants that came to America after WWI. Nick had been born in Norway, while Ruth was born in America three years later. The patriarch of the family, Oscar Nelson, had come from a long-line of ancestors that were woodsmen back in the Old Country. In his youth he had married a beautiful young Norwegian gal, Helen Person, and with their first child Nick in tow, they had immigrated to America with dreams of tall timberlands and easy pickings for the strong and knowledgeable lumberjacks like Oscar.

They had started out in the forest of Wisconsin, where Ruth had been born. Here Oscar struggled with his new English language and the forest methods of his adopted new home. He was a socialist, loud and proud, which was not well received by most of the free-spirited lumberjacks of America. Oscar was bullheaded and belligerent and he made few friends. So, ever so slowly, the Nelson family moved from one lumber camp to the next. Always heading west and never looking back. In less than five years they found themselves in the Redwood Forest camps of Northern California. It was here that his accident happened: a large redwood limb came crashing down from a giant sequoia breaking his right leg and shattering one ankle. The forest camp he was working at was forty miles away from the closest town. He almost died on his journey searching for a doctor, but he didn't. Instead, he would have a limp leg for the rest of his life. This accident took away his days in the forest and filled his head with anger and self-pity. During his long recovery he became reliant on opium and whiskey to kill the pain and the humiliation. Oscar would never be the same again. His dark days and long nights had just started. Thank God for his wife Helen, she became the matriarch that saved her family from starving during the Great Depression.

Hebo wasn't much of a village, just a gas station, tavern and hardware store with a handful full of other businesses, mostly related to farming. The reason for the little hamlet was the junction of County Highway 22 with the Coast Highway 101, north or south. The Hebo Café, next to the intersection, was the gathering place for most of the local community. This was a small town where everyone knew their neighbor's business and who was doing what.

Ruth pulled her bike into the Café parking lot about 7:30 AM. The restaurant had just opened and there were a few cars parked outside. Using her kick stand, she rested her bike upright next to the front door and carefully removed her eggs from the basket. Once inside, she was greeted by an older woman, taking a food order at the counter with order pad in hand.

"Right on time Ruthie," she said with a smile. "We were down to our last few eggs. Take them into the kitchen before Herb starts complaining."

Ruth nodded a warm smile back to the woman and headed for the swinging doors to the rear kitchen. "Is Lucy coming in this morning?" she asked.

"Yes," the older lady answered, "but she's running a little late."

The Wilson family, Herb, Alice and their daughter Lucy ran the Hebo Café. It was open from 7AM to 3PM six days a week. The restaurant was small but clean, with just a dozen stools at the counter and six tables with bentwood chairs on one side of the room. The food was good and the coffee pot was always on, but breakfast and lunch was all they served. Working at the Café was hard work and Ruth helped out occasionally for extra money.

Moving inside the spotless kitchen, Ruth put half her eggs in a wire basket next to the flat-top grill and the other half on a shelf next to the prep area.

"How many eggs did you bring us?" Herb asked gruffly wearing his usual white cook's apron with food stains and blood. He was a fireplug of a man with tattooed arms as thick as his thighs and a face in a perpetual frown. Herb had learned to cook in the Navy and now he supported his family as one of the best short-order cooks on the coast. With his physical size and tattoos, he looked quite menacing, but deep-down Herb was as soft as pussy-cat.

"Six dozen this morning," Ruth answered shyly.

"Is that damn mangy mutt of yours in my restaurant? I don't like him mingling with my customers."

Ruth forced a smile on her face, "He's tied up in the parking lot. I know you love my dog Mr. Wilson; you're always feeding him kitchen scraps."

He glanced at her from his grill. "Never fried up dog meat before, but the Chinese say it's delicious. I might make room for him on my grill one of these days."

"No you won't" Ruth nodded with a smile. "Winnie and I are going to town today so I better get a move on."

Mr. Wilson flipped six fried eggs at once without breaking a yoke. "Give my best to your mother. Alice will give you the egg money and be careful out there it's a long bike ride to town."

Ruth sat down at an empty stool out front. Before she was settled, Alice slid a cup of hot coffee in front of her. The place was busy, but not swamped.

"How many eggs today sweetie?" she asked. Alice was the complete opposite of her husband; she was thin like a string bean and as friendly as a preacher. Her brown hair had streaks of gray and she wore the same pink pinstriped uniform with a white hanky every day. Alice was the face of the restaurant, she took the orders, served the meals and managed the cash register. Nothing got by her, she knew all the Tillamook County gossip and dispensed more news than the local weekly newspaper.

"Six dozen today," Ruth answered. "Mom wanted me to tell you that the new curtains for the windows will be done tomorrow. She'll come by in the afternoon to put them up."

Alice moved to the cash register and pushed the 'No

Sale' key. The machine rang a bell and the cash drawer opened. She removed $1.44 and placed the money in front of Ruth.

"Can't get rich on 2 cents an egg honey, but it's a start," she said with a smile. "Do you want to work a couple hours today?"

"I was hoping not too. I have some business in town," Ruth told her. "But if you're shorthanded I'll help out."

"Not a problem," Alice answered. "What kind of business? It's a long way to town on a bike."

Ruth hesitated answering her question. She knew all too well that whatever she told her would be all over town before the sun went down. But the Wilson's were good friends and she needed to say something.

"I'm going to take the driver's license test at the courthouse. Father finally fixed our tractor and he wants me to learn how to drive it."

"Didn't Nick do the plowing last year?"

"Yes," Ruth answered. "Guess I'm the new man around the house now."

"With the war on, it's a good idea to know how to drive," Alice answered. "You should be coming back this way before we close, so please stop by so I'll know you made it home safely."

Just then the front door opened and Lucy came in the Café. "Sorry I'm late mom, dad asked me to pick up some more ground pork and the butcher was late opening up."

Lucy Wilson and Ruth were good friends. They were in the same graduating class at Cloverdale School.

There were only seven students in the senior class this year: three boys and four girls. The boys were excited about joining the military after high school and killing Japs, while the girls wanted to find good jobs or maybe a husband before they went off to war. That $10,000 Government Life Insurance Policy sounded pretty good, to a lot of people, just coming out of the Great Depression.

When Lucy saw Ruth at the counter she came over and gave her a hug. She was also wearing a pinstriped uniform just like her mothers. Ruth had one as well, hanging up in the kitchen. But she didn't like to wear it; it was too girly for her.

"Are we working together?" Lucy hopefully asked.

"No," her mother answered. "Ruthie has business in town today. Maybe tomorrow: we need to get that cooler cleaned out."

Ruth and Lucy had coffee, talking and giggling about their upcoming graduation. There was going to be a dance after the ceremonies and neither of them could think of any school boy they would want to dance with. "All they talk about is the damn war or their damn crops," Ruth said shaking her head. "I wish my brother Nick was home, I'd dance with him."

"So would I," Lucy quickly replied. "We have slim pickings when comes to country boys. What we need is a real man!"

With that comment, the front door opened again and in stepped a young man wearing the blue and black uniform of a Tillamook County Deputy Sheriff. "Who owns the pug mutt tied up outside?" He yelled to the room with authority.

Ruth stood from her stool and turned to him. "I do,"

she answered. "What's the problem?"

"Your dog is all tangled up in his leash howling like wolf. He's bothering my dog; you need to get him to calm down."

Gathering up her egg money, Ruth followed the officer outside and as she did, she noticed his name tag pinned to his uniform, Officer Roy Adams. He was tall and slender with a gun on his hip and a felt, campaign hat on his head. Roy looked strong, handsome and young!

Once in the parking lot Ruth noticed a county Studebaker pickup truck with a German Shepherd peering out the passenger window. She had her eyes fixed on Winnie who was indeed tangled up and howling loudly. Ruth rushed to him and untangled his lead. Scratching his ears, she said, "Don't think my dog is the problem here. Looks like your pooch might be in heat."

The deputy shook his head sheepishly, "They both just went wild when they saw each other."

"Don't worry about it," Ruth answered coyly. "Your dog is about four hands tall, while my mine is just under two hands. That's a tall hump for my stubby-legged little Winnie here. So I don't think there's going to be any puppies in their future."

"Winnie, what a funny name for a dog: why do you call him that?"

"Winston Churchill," Ruth answered. "What's your bitch's name?"

"Fang, she's a guard dog out on the county farm."

When Winnie calmed down Ruth lifted him inside her basket. "Sorry if he frightened, your vicious guard dog," Ruth said with a smile. "We are on our way to town, so she'll get over it."

"You must be a farm girl to know such things," the deputy said.

"Well, I'm no stranger to the barnyard sir," she replied remounting her bicycle. "See you down the road deputy," Ruth nodded, with her eyes flirting, as she pedaled away.

Leaving Roy flatfooted he yelled out to her, "What's your name girl?"

"Ruthie," she shouted back.

"Ruthie who?" he yelled back

"Nelson."

With her dog in the basket and her bike wheels turning without the playing cards, Ruth apologized to him for disturbing his romance, "She just wasn't the right size for you Winnie. You need something smaller."

The dog cocked his head as if he understood.

Pedaling for town, she turned north on the coast highway. The asphalt roadway was much better than the oiled county road she had arrived on. It was a smooth ride with wide graveled shoulders on both sides of the highway. It was twenty miles to the courthouse in the town of Tillamook; it would take her more than two hours of hard peddling to get there. But the weather was clear and warm and the traffic lite, other than the many big log trucks going her way.

Before she had left the café Mr. Wilson had made her a sack lunch of a tuna fish sandwich and potato fries. He had also put some kitchen scraps in her sack for her dog. He was all bluster when it came to Winnie. He loved her dog.

As she rode, and walked her bike, the countryside reminded her of Wisconsin forest lands that stretched out as far as the eye could see. But the Oregon trees, primarily the Douglas-fir, seemed straighter, taller and thicker than those she remembered back east. There was something majestic about these Oregon trees; they were so green and beautiful, Gods miracle at His best.

Then her thoughts turned to the miracle of her mother Helen, she was the hand of God raising her family. She had been born into a frugal Norwegian family that believed in waste not, want not, and spend not. Hard work and frugality were the true ways to comfort and security. "Never lend, nor borrow, what you do not need," she loved to say to whoever would listen.

After her husband's accident, and during his long recovery, Helen revealed to her family that over the last five years of coming to America she had saved over three hundred dollars in a coffee can! She had accomplished this amazing task by working in the dining rooms, kitchens and sculleries of the many lumber camps where Oscar had worked. With her savings, and what remained of his earnings, the family had saved enough money to purchase the family farm that Ruth now called Shangri-La. It had once belonged to a family of loggers, but had burned down in a forest fire. The Nelson family had purchased the twenty acres, sight unseen, and rebuilt the farm from the ground up. But that was fourteen years ago and now the family worried about farming with the world at war. What was their path to comfort and security?

Oscar, with his gimpy leg, could no longer work in

the forest. While he could walk some and do light tasks, there were just no jobs for him harvesting timber. So, he reinvented himself as a Shingle Weaver. At the lumber mill cedar bolts would be cut to length and he would hand-split these lengths into cedar shingles. Using just a splitting froe and a hatchet Oscar would sit on a log stump for hours, splitting, sizing and trimming shakes into wood bundles that would cover twenty-five square feet of a cedar roof or siding. He was paid by the bundles he made, fifty cents each! Every bundle was stacked with his mark burned into the wood strapping. On a good day he could stack twenty bundles. Ten dollars a day that was good money! But it was tiresome and humiliating work for a proud Norwegian lumberjack. Oscar hated his job, and on paydays he often drank and gambled away most of his purse. When sober, Oscar was a craftsman, when inebriated he was the town drunk. Most of the community looked the other way when he approached or whispered under their breath about the tragic sadness of the Nelson family. This was one of the many reasons why Nick had enlisted right out of high school. He was embarrassed by his father's notorious reputation.

**A Silhouette Appeared in the Sunrise**

## Chapter Two

***Munson Creek Incident***

About halfway to town Ruth stopped pedaling when she approached Munson Creek. The sun was bright and warm with Winnie panting and his tongue drooling out of the side of his mouth. It was time for more water and something to eat. The crystal-clear creek looked like a good place for a picnic. As she walked her bike to the guardrail and used her kick-stand, two log trucks rambled by and gave her a blast with their air horns. With their trailers stacked high with freshly harvested logs, both drivers waved at her with big smiles and she waved back. These log trucks and their cargo, were a vivid reminder of the richness and beauty of the surrounding forest.

Sliding down the grass embankment alongside the road, with her sack-lunch in hand, the girl and her dog moved towards the creek bed. The underbrush was just coming to life with signs of new growth and many shades of color. Both sides of the stream had young saplings growing at the water's edge as it raced over the rocks and boulders making a gurgling sound. Kneeling by the water, Ruth removed her straw hat, allowing her long blond hair to fall to her shoulders. Taking sandwiches in hand, she shared one with Winnie and watched him eat. He didn't much like tuna fish but on this morning, he ate it with gusto. After Ruth finished her sandwich, she splashed water on her sweaty face and cupped her hands, drinking the water. As she did so, Winnie drank next to her lapping up his share of the brook. When he finished, he made a beeline for the grass embankment to take care of business.

As Ruth drank the cool, clear, sweet water, she became mesmerized with the sheer beauty of the location. Looking upstream she could see the many small waterfalls, like stepping stones, stacked on top of each other with a canopy of green tree limbs as far up the creek as she could see. The setting was fresh and cool like a picture in a magazine.

She took one more sip of water and then it happened! What was stunning and beautiful one moment was now bleak and dark. Out of nowhere, someone behind her grabbed her hair and pushed her, face down, into the waters of the creek. She landed hard on the wet rocks with her clothes becoming sopping wet. Spread out on the water, she struggled to regain reality. What had happened and why? Slowly, she rolled over and found, what appeared to be, a giant of a man standing over her.

"What the hell do we have here?" he yelled at her. "You're just a golden mermaid in my creek!"

Ruth was stunned and confused as she struggled to get to her feet on the slippery wet rocks. He was big and ugly with glaring eyes and a frightening scowl. He wore a dirty striped uniform of a prisoner without any restraints.

"I love little girls in wet clothes. We're going have a good time honey."

Ruth finally got to her feet, as frightened as she had ever been! Her eyes darted around the water bed looking for help, that's when she noticed a fat short stick stuck in the mud. She picked it up for protection using both hands and yelled out for her dog with panic in her voice. "Winnie help!"

The man, ankle deep in the water, splashed towards her with a sadistic grin. "You going to come after me with that little stick honey?" he asked her sarcastically. "My prick is bigger than your stick. You're going to enjoy it!"

Winnie came running back to the stream barking as loud as he could. Ruth raised the stick overhead, ready to swing at her attacker.

"That little dog don't bother me none," the prisoner said with lechery on his face. "After we're done, I'll kill him… just for the fun of it."

That's when she heard another loud voice, "Get him Fang," with a gun shot into the air that echoed down the creek.

"You touch that girl convict and you're a dead man," the man yelled with a pistol in hand.

His voice and the gun shot startled Ruth and the prisoner. They both turned his direction and Ruth saw Officer Roy Adams rushing down the embankment with his dog in the lead.

In the blink of an eye, Fang raced to the water growling and howling then jumped onto the back of the prisoner. Both man and dog fell into the water as Ruth moved quickly for the shore. The next thing she knew Deputy Adams was standing next to her calling off his dog. As Fang finally let loose of the prisoners bleeding leg, Officer Adams removed a whistle from his pocket and blew it three times. The harsh shrieking sounds of the whistle startled Ruth even more with tears and fear in her eyes and her hands trembling.

"It's all over Ruthie," the deputy said wading into the creek and placing handcuffs on the convicts hands. "Mr. Maggot here is one of our prison laborers working in the woods. He runs away occasionally, but we always gather him back up. Don't let him scare you, he's all talk."

Ruth took a deep breath, trying to recover her wits. "What laborers and how did you find me?"

The deputy helped his prisoner to his feet with his leg still dripping with blood.

"Simple enough, I saw your bicycle up on the road. Didn't you see our warning signs up there: 'Convicts Working in the Woods?"

"No," Ruth answered with a frown. "I was busy having a picnic with my dog."

The sounds of another whistle rolled through the creek bed with two more deputies and another dog running their way. As they waited for their arrival, Officer Adams explained that because of the shortage of able-bodied men the county used convict labor working in the woods to clean up the forest underbrush. "They help us prevent forest fires," Roy said. "It's one of the many ways we prepare for the wild fire season around here. Mr. Maggot is a good worker. But he has a love hate complex, when it comes to pretty young girls."

"What's he in jail for?"

"Beating-up a husband, who was beating-up his wife...go figure?"

"He called me a golden mermaid among other things: he scared the crap out of me." She said with a small grin of confidence returning to her face.

"It's all over, don't let this sack of shit scare you. I'll drive you to town. It will give you some time to dry off your clothes and I'll get to know you better.

"Are you a rookie cop? I've never seen your face before?" Ruth asked, still a little dazed.

Roy shook his head with a grin. "I was six months ago when I joined the force, now I'm a seasoned veteran who likes to know all the pretty girls in my county."

"Are you flirting with me Officer Adams?"

"No, I don't think so. I'm just doing my duty."

That ended the Munson Creek incident, but not the nightmares that would surely follow.

With the bicycle in the back of the pickup and Ruth in the passenger seat, fanning her damp overalls in the warm air of the open window, Roy drove the truck north on highway 101. In between driver and passenger sat Winnie with a happy face. Fang, the German Shepherd, and Mr. Maggot the convict, had been handed off to the other two deputy sheriff's working at the camp.

"How old are you?" Officer Adams asked the girl with his hands on the steering wheel.

She kept fanning herself and lied back to him without hesitation, “Seventeen.”

He looked at her with curious eyes, “And where’s your farm?”

“Half mile south of the Cloverdale school on the county road. I’m graduating high school there next week. How old are you, Roy?” Ruth asked with her blue eyes sparkling.

He frowned from the wheel without taking his eyes off the road. “Twenty-three, and I know your next question: why aren't I in the Army?”

Ruth chuckled, “That wasn’t my next question. Where are you from?”

Roy glanced at her, “That’s everyone’s second question. The Army turned me down, I’m 4F. I tried them all: Navy, Marines, Army and even the Coast Guard. They all turned me away.”

Ruth could see shame in his face. This was a sore subject for him and she hesitated in asking why.

“So where are you from?” She asked again giving him her full attention.

Officer Roy Adams was the oldest son of Sheriff William Adams; he had been born and raised in Tillamook County. When Roy was just little tyke, he had come down with rheumatic fever and nearly died. It was because of this old fever that the military had turned him down. Roy graduated from high school in 1939 and attended Oregon State University with an eye on a forestry degree. But with the dark days of war looming, he dropped out of college and tried to enlist. Finally, when his Draft Board issued him a 4F rating, he gave up hope and became deputy sheriff working for his father. Roy felt cheated that he couldn't be a warrior for his country, so he took the recommendation of his Draft Board and became a policeman as his part in the war effort.

Ruth was fascinated with his story and kept her eyes fixated on his dimpled chin. She respected him and his determination to do his part. Now here was a man she would dance with at her graduation party. She would even consider wearing a dress, but she didn't have the courage to ask him. He was too handsome and out of her league. But everyone could dream.

**Zeppelins**

As the Studebaker approached the town of Tillamook there is a long gentle slope that is the gateway to the Tillamook Valley. Here the landscape is dotted with family farms with mostly livestock of dairy cows and cattle. Once on the valley floor, where a small municipal airport used to be, there was now a sprawling Navy Air Station. Ruth had read about the construction of the gigantic blimp hangars in the newspaper, but this was the first time she had seen the blimps and the Quonset hut style hanger's close-up. And what a sight it was! As they slowly drove by the station, Roy was big-eyed spouting out information like a news story. Each of the two wooden hangers were the largest free-standing, clear-span, wooden structures in the world! They covered more than seven acres each, with the two buildings over a thousand feet long, three hundred feet wide and with blimp docking towers fifteen stories tall. Each hanger was being constructed with over two million board feet of lumber.

When completed, the two hangers could hold eight K-class blimps for anti-submarine patrol and convoy escort duty. Each airship contained 425,000 cubic feet of helium and could carry a crew and armaments of about eight thousand pounds.

**During World War II, 134 K-class blimps were built and configured for patrol and anti-submarine warfare operations. The blimps were 1,072 feet long, 296 feet wide, and towered more than 15 stories high.**

"How fast can a blimp fly?" Ruth asked with her overwhelming views.

Roy pulled over to the shoulder of the road and stopped, "One of the pilots told me about 80 knots and they can cover almost 15,000 square miles a day.

Ruth stared up at one of the blimps attached to a docking tower. "They are so big and clumsy looking. How do they protect themselves?"

After lighting a cigarette, Roy pulled back on to the highway. "From what I understand they don't have much protection. A few machine guns, fore and aft and a radio to call for help."

As they passed the Air Station Ruth noticed all the uniformed men working on the tarmac. "That's a lot of sailors at work. How many men do they have?"

Roy shook his head sadly, "My father told me that Squadron ZP-33 will have a full complement of men, over a thousand sailors. I wish I was one of them."

"Buck-up Roy, you're doing your part. Thanks for putting up with all my questions and saving my virtue back at the creek."

He smiled broadly, "All in a good day's work."

Roy pulled his pick-up truck into the rear parking lot of the courthouse and showed Ruth to the rear entrance of the basement. With Winnie on a leash, they walked past a few desks and turned down a few halls until they came to a closed door with Oregon Motor Vehicles stenciled on the frosted glass. Opening this door, Roy and Ruth went inside the office. The room was small with only two middle aged women working at wooden desks across from each other. Both the ladies greeted Roy with big smiles and Ruth with curious glances.

"Good morning ladies, I bring you a customer for your famous driver's test," he said in a joyful voice. "I found Ruth here, and her dog, having a picnic up on Munson Creek this morning. Unfortunately, one of our convicts tried to have his way with her. Fang stopped him of course. So, take good care of her, she's little shaken up."

Obviously, Roy and the ladies were good friends and Ruth rolled her eyes as he went from desk-to-desk hugging both women while continuing to talk.

Finally, Ruth interrupted him. "Where's the little

girls room please?" She asked shyly. One lady, who Roy called Mildred, gave her bathroom directions. "When you come back honey, we'll give you the test."

In the ladies room, Ruth brushed out her hair and cleaned up her overalls the best she could. Then she took care of business and started out for the office again. That's when she noticed a public bulletin board in the hallway. She stopped and read a few postings. One typed out message caught her eye: **Fire Lookouts Wanted for Summer Season. $2.00 a day, plus keep. See Chief Forester Eric Jacobs, at the firehouse for details.** She had no idea what 'keep' meant, but this looked like a great summer job, so Ruth took the message off the board and put it in her pocket.

When she returned to the office, Roy and the other lady were gone. Only Mildred was waiting with a copy of the test on her desk. When Ruth looked at her application, she was surprised to see it was partially filled out with her name, age and rural address.

"Did you bring your birth certificate honey?" Mildred asked.

"No," she answered shaking her head. "I was born in a logging camp in Wisconsin. Never did get a birth certificate." As she lied about her age again, she noticed the application listed her age at seventeen! All was well!

"That's alright honey," Mildred answered. "Roy vouched for you and that's good enough for me."

Ruth grinned at Mildred, "Sure you can trust him."

"Yes, I think I can," she answered smiling back. "After all, he's, my son."

Ruth was surprised again, "You're married to the Sheriff and the mother of Deputy Roy?"

"Yes, I am," Mildred said proudly. "He's my little boy."

Ruth took the test with Winnie curled-up on her high-tops. It wasn't hard as she had read the manual a couple of times before coming to town. As she finished up with the last few questions her head was still spinning about the nepotism of the Adams family. How sweet is that to have three government jobs?

Mildred corrected her test right after she finished. Her final score: 98%. She only missed two questions: one about hand signals when turning and stopping and the other question about when to use a red flag with oversized loads. Ruth was delighted with the outcome.

"Do you have a car?" Mildred asked typing out her driver's license.

"No," she answered. "That's next on my list. I've got to get my bicycle from Roy's truck do you know when his coming back?"

Mildred stopped typing Ruth's license and rubber-stamped it a few times. "That will be two dollars for your license honey. Roy had to take a prisoner to the county farm; he should be back in hour or so."

Ruth paid her from the egg money and a dollar bill she had in her pocket. "Please tell Roy that we're across the street at the firehouse with the Chief Forester."

Mildred nodded with a grin, "You come back and see me anytime honey."

**Tillamook Chief Forester Badge**

# Chapter Three

## Chief Forester

With her new license safely in her pocket, Ruth and Winnie crossed the street in front of the courthouse to the fire station. As she did, her day dreams were about what kind of a used car she could buy after working all summer as a fire lookout. A station wagon would be nice and could help out around the farm, but a 1937 Ford Coupe had also caught her eye. Time would tell, maybe she could buy an all-yellow car with white wall tires. That would be real jake!

Once in the firehouse, she had to search out the County Forester Office which she finally found on the third floor overlooking the parked fire trucks. His office was tiny, about the size of a double closet, with pictures all over his walls. The Chief Forester himself, Mr. Eric Jacobs, was a tall muscular fellow with graying sideburns and a firm handshake. The forester had a welcoming smile with a weathered complexion and dusty red hair. He invited Ruth to take a seat, in front of his desk, which she did, as it was the only other chair in his office.

Ruth showed him the card from the bulletin board,

"Mr. Jacobs, I'd like to have this job. Is it still open?"

He looked her over carefully, "People just call me Eric or Chief. I'm the Forester responsible for all the forests in Tillamook County and a few other surrounding counties as well. What I fear the most is wildfires, like the big burn of 34. Yes, the job is still open, but let me tell you about it before you fill out an application."

That's how it all started with Chief Jacobs outlining in great detail the responsibilities of fire lookouts. He showed her forest maps, with pictures of firefighters working in the flames. "Our smoke-jumpers are experts at containing and putting out fires. They go into the remote locations on primitive roads and trails and sometimes they parachute into the fires as well."

He had more pictures on the wall of the tall log towers with small houses on top. "This is where our lookouts live and work 24/7 watching out for smoke and flames. The way to prevent wild fires is to get to the small fires first before they become wild."

Ruth was amazed to learn the job was a 'live-in' kind of opportunity. "So I don't go home at night?"

"Nope," The Chief answered. "Think of it as living in the clouds."

He told her the job was lonely and remote with her eyes always on the alert and her nose and mind always searching for smoke. "These watch towers are not tree houses; they are one of the many tools we use in helping prevent forest fires. You have to live on your own, cook your own meals and coexist with a forest teaming with wild animals. This is a dangerous business and you don't want to end up in the middle of a wild fire."

Ruth had questions: "When does the fire season start and end?

"June first, through late September or early October: given weather conditions."

Ruth counted the days in her head. "We get paid $2.00 every day?"

"Yes," he answered. "Plus keep."

"What is keep," she asked.

"I bring out food and supplies twice a month, to 'keep' you fed and alert about what's going on in your section of the forest."

The Chief asked her questions as well, "Can you cook for yourself and camp-out alone? Are you any good with math? Do you know how to use a gun… do you know how to use a compass…what about shortwave radios, have you ever used one?"

Ruth shaded the truth again by answering all his questions in the affirmative. She had read a few books about living in a wilderness, but never expected to have to do it herself. She would have to read up on how to survive.

"With the war on, I'm having a hard time finding lookouts this season," Eric said reaching for an application form. You seem strong enough and smart enough to do the job, but are you mature enough to live only by your own wits?"

"I can," Ruth answered with a determined face. "My family has worked in the woods all of my life. I'm the girl for this job."

Then the Chief asked her if she had a driver's license? Perfect timing! Proudly she handed her new license to the Chief. He glanced at it with a smile that turned into a frown and he handed it back to her. “Sorry Miss Nelson, I can’t use you.”

“Why,” she asked sharply. “Because I’m a girl?”

“No,” the Chief replied firmly. “We’ve had female fire lookouts since the war of 1812. It’s because you’re only seventeen, and the county has a rule that all employees must be eighteen years old or older.”

His words felt like a gut kick from a mule. This just couldn’t be, all of her dreams would be for not. Another year of riding Nicks bicycle just wasn’t right. *Now what*? Her mind yelled.

“How about if we get a waiver signed by her parents?” Roy’s voice said.

Ruth turned quickly in her chair and found Roy standing behind her with a big smile on his face. “Then we take the waiver to the County Commissioners as a hardship because of the war. There are just not enough experienced able-bodied people to go around.”

Eric liked the idea and agreed. “That just might work… but let’s not get our hopes up until we see what the Commissioners have to say.”

Ruth filled out a job application while Roy typed out a waiver for her parents to sign. As it turned out, Roy and Eric were old friends; the Deputy himself had been a fire lookout in the summer after his graduation from high school.

Ruth glared fondly at Roy; he had appeared again just in time to save her bacon. She was impressed. Maybe their friendship was meant to be?

As they finished up with the Chief, Ruth finally

faced up to a little reality. "I don't really know much about shortwave radios sir. Sorry I said I did."

"That's alright," he replied. "The Navy is going to teach us about our new radios. This year we'll have communications with the Air Station. If we have any really big fires the Navy blimps are going to help us douse them out."

After the Chief finished typing the waiver he let Roy read it. He nodded his approval and handed it to Ruth.

"I'll come by your farm on Monday morning to pick up the signed waiver," he said with a hopeful smile. "We should have an answer from the Commissioners within the week."

Roy walked her to his truck, "Mom said you were looking for your bike, but I don't think you'll need it."

"Why not?" Ruth asked.

"I'm going back to the convict camp with some medical supplies. Guess Fang took a bigger chunk out of Mr. Maggot's leg then I thought. You can ride along."

You keep helping me, why?"

"It must be your charming personality," Roy replied, opening the passenger door with a smile. "Riding with me is better than pedaling with your dog in the basket."

Ruth lifted Winnie onto the bench seat…"Can I drive?"

"I don't think so," he answered gesturing her into the cab. "Have you ever driven a stick shift before?"

"Yes many times," she said confidently. "Our tractor is a stick shift so I know all about the clutch."

"We'll see down road," Roy answered, getting into

the driver's side.

As they drove out of town Ruth poked some fun at Roy, "All of your family works for the government. That's good work if you can get it."

Roy frowned, "We all march to a different drummer. Dad works for the voters, mom works for the state and I work for the county, it seems normal to us."

"Do you have any more nepotism at home?" Ruth asked jokingly.

"Yes," Roy answered smiling. "My younger sister Ellen: She wants to be a Navy WAVE, but she's only 12 years old. We believe in nepotism, it puts bread on our table."

Approaching the Naval Air Station again, Roy changed the subject giving Ruth some cautionary comments. He told her there were only five Watch Towers for all of the forests of Tillamook County and that the towers had been built by the Civilian Conservation Corps ten years before. "They are all alike, only some towers are taller than others. The huts, or nests, are all alike as well, with only about 300 square feet of living space with a wood burning stove, one small table and a chair, windows all around and one hardwood platform to sleep on with your sleeping bag. There is no electricity, no running water and just a one hole outhouse on the ground level. Oh yes, in the middle of your tiny room is the Fire Finder, a large device used to pin point fires. Your nest can be as hot as an oven in the daytime and as cold as an igloo at night. This is primitive living, at its best."

Ruth listened to Roy's comments with her eyes wide and her mouth open. What she was hearing sounded like a great adventure.

"If you get a chance to select your tower, ask for Hebo Butte," Roy continued. "That was my tower five years ago, and I made a few changes to it for better living."

"Like what?" Rut asked.

"Hebo Butte is a 40 foot tall tower so I installed a hand cranked lift to bring up supplies, firewood and water. I also got a mattress up there for better sleeping. Hebo Lake is nearby for drinking and bathing, but it's a mile walk back to the nest with your drinking water. Then there are the wild animals: deer, elk, cougars and bears, to name but a few. These aren't soft and fuzzy creatures from the barnyard."

"It sounds charming to me," Ruth said. "Like a Jack London novel,"

"Don't get your hopes up Ruthie. You still have to convince your parents and the County Commissioners. If it was up to me, I'd say no."

"Well thank goodness it's not up to you," she answered with a determined face.

It was lunch time when they pulled into the Convict Camp. It wasn't much of a place, just a flat spot next to the road with a nearby brook and set-up with two army tents and cooking fires. There were about a dozen convicts, all dressed in their dirty striped uniforms, sitting on stumps and log snags eating a hot meal with three guards and two dogs watching.

Roy pulled into the camp and parked. That's when Winnie saw Fang again and he started whimpering. Ruth distracted him to quiet him down. Soon she noticed Mr. Maggot looking at her from his bowl of beans with a lecherous smile. The thought of violence raced through her head with all the prisoners seemingly gawking at her. Fear melted her resolve.

"I'll stay in the truck," she said glaring at Roy as he slipped out of the driver's side with the medical supplies.

"Not a problem Ruthie," he replied smiling. "I'll check out Maggot's leg and we'll be on our way. You can drive us to Hebo."

With that invitation, Ruth's mind set went from convicts to clutches. She moved her dog over and slid behind the wheel. She waited and watched patiently as Roy doctored Maggot's leg. *Come on, hurry up, I want to get out of here*, was the only thought she held in her head.

**Fingers Crossed**

When Roy returned to his truck the prisoners were just lining up for the count and going back to work. As the men waited, with tools in hand, they all seemed to be glaring at Ruth. She would have none of their looks and looked away as Roy took the passenger seat giving her instructions on how to start the motor. She turned the key and the engine purred. Then he showed her how to find reverse on the gearshift and told her how to gently use the clutch. It sounds so simple, but it wasn't. The truck lunged backwards just missing a guard rail, with Ruth slamming on the brakes and shifting into low gear with the transmission grinding and the wheels spinning.

The prisoners started laughing and yelling, "Watch out women driver, get a horse lady, no backseat driving… she's out to get us!"

"Gently, like a baby," Roy said firmly as she moved onto the highway. "Watch out for log trucks."

Like a bucking bronco, the Studebaker lunged forward, backfired and lunged forward again. Roy held his breath and his temper. "Gently with those pedals, this isn't a tractor plowing a field."

Even Winnie jumped off the bench seat to hide under Roy's legs. He was no fool!

"I'm trying," Ruth yelled back at him, clearly frustrated.

Slowly, ever so slowly, with gears grinding, Ruth got the feel of the transmission and smoothed out the ride with the convicts still watching in her rearview mirror. She was embarrassed and had tears in eyes. "It sounded so simple in the books," she finally said.

Roy could breathe again. "It's just like real life… expect the unexpected."

In a calming voice, he gave her some driving tips and told her that in becoming a Deputy Sheriff he had to go to a special driving school for police officers. "It takes time and confidence with lots of practice. You'll get the hang of it."

After a few moments of utter panic, Ruth was in control of the truck and heading for Hebo. Even Winnie had jumped back-up to the bench seat.

"I have a confession," Roy said watching Ruth at the wheel. "I should have told you this earlier today."

She glanced at him with a curious expression and then turned her eyes back on the road. "You have a wife or a girlfriend?"

"No, well maybe I do. I had a girlfriend in college, but she's working at the Kaiser Shipyards in Portland now. That's not my confession. I had a run-in with your father

Oscar a few days ago. I was sent out to a drunk and disorderly call at the Ship Ahoy Tavern at 10 o'clock in the morning. Oscar was preaching the benefits of socialism to an angry crowd of morning drinkers. A barroom brawl was about to begin, so I tried to get him to stop talking. In the process of our scuffle he took a swing at me and missed, and I took a swing at him and didn't miss. I knocked him out cold right there on the tavern floor, didn't mean to hit him so hard, but I did. That's my confession. I didn't realize he was a cripple until I got him back on his feet."

Ruth smiled with both hands on the wheel. "So that's where his black eye came from. He told me he got the shiner by tripping over his gimpy leg. Did you arrest him?"

"No," Roy answered firmly. "I put him in the cooler with a half-pot of black coffee. I let him go home in the afternoon. He was sober as a temperance meeting. Thought you should know this, your father doesn't like me very much."

Ruth chuckled reaching for her courage. "Don't worry about it. He blacks-out when he drinks. He won't remember a thing about that day. But I do have a favor to ask: will you come to my graduation party dance? It's a week from today, at 7 o'clock at the Cloverdale School?"

Roy was hesitant, what could he say? He felt guilty about cold-cocking a cripple like Oscar. That was more like being a bully then a police officer. So he agreed to come to the party. "I'm not much of a dancer, but I'll do my best," he answered as Ruth pulled into the Hebo Café parking lot. "Do you want me in my uniform or civilian clothes?"

She turned off the ignition and turned his way with her eyes glowing. “Uniform please, you’re so handsome in blue and black.”

With Winnie in the basket, the bike ride home seemed like an eternity; so much had happened that day. Now Ruth faced just one more hurdle: getting her parents to sign-off on the County Waiver so she could become a Firewatcher.

Ruth had taken Roy inside the Café and had introduced him to the Wilson’s. They all had coffee together and talked about the upcoming graduation party. Lucy seemed jealous that Ruth had spent all day with such a handsome man and that he had agreed to come to the dance. Roy promised Lucy that he would save her a couple of dances and she swooned all over him.

Roy and Ruth parted where it had all started that morning, in the parking lot. He offered to drive her home, but she turned him down wanting some time to map-out her strategy with her parents. Her mother Helen, shouldn't be a problem, but her father Oscar would be, especially if he was drunk. The task at hand was to pray for a sober father.

It was getting late in the afternoon when she turned off the county road and down the dirt driveway to Shangri-La. The house and barn glittered in the sun. She could smell the farmyard and hear the livestock in the fields. She had chores to do: gathering more eggs, slopping the pigs and milking the cows. With Nick gone, all his chores were now on her shoulders. But before she went to work Ruth would soften-up her mother with all the news of her day.

Ruth walked her bike to the barn and lifted Winnie out of the basket. Once on the ground he strutted around the barnyard like a conquering hero. Resting her bicycle against the barn walls she turned for the porch and entered the kitchen through the backdoor. Here she found her mother Helen preparing the evening meal.

"I was getting worried about you! You started off so early this morning." Helen said looking up from chopping vegetables on a wooden cutting board. She was a short gal with dusty blond hair and deep set blue eyes. In her late thirties, Helen still looked like the copper skin beauty she once was. Men still turned her way and Oscar still got jealous of them.

"Did you tell Alice that I'd bring her curtains in tomorrow?"

Ruth nodded yes, "I got my driver's license mom and I drove partway home."

Helen stopped chopping and looked at her daughter with an inquisitive glare. "How did that happen and what did you drive?"

That started the conversation between mother and daughter about the day's events. Ruth told her with glee almost everything, from the egg money to meeting Deputy Sheriff Roy Adams and from the driver's test to her driving partway home from town. She left out the details about Mr. Maggot and the convict camp. No need to get her mom all worked up.

"I've invited Officer Roy to my graduation party and he's coming! Lucy is so jealous that I asked him first. I told him to wear his uniform: he is such nice looking man."

"And what are you going to wear?" Helen asked with a smile. "I'm sure this nice looking man isn't use to dancing with girls in baggy hand-me-down overalls. Is it time for me to make you a proper dress?"

This was typical Helen; she was a gifted seamstress, making clothes and other things for family and friends. She even took in laundry for extra money. She worked like a slave, and saved like a miser, with a rusting coffee can as the family bank.

"Yes," Ruth answered with a perplexed frown. "Yes I'll wear a dress to graduation, but nothing to flashy, just something simple."

Helen returned to chopping, she handled the butcher knife like an expert cutting up the meat for a stew. "My little girl has her first boyfriend, how sweet is this!"

"Please mom, I don't have a boyfriend. Roy is just a nice guy in a uniform that let me drive his pick-up back from town."

"Did he try to steal a kiss?"

Ruth shook her head, "No! But the County offered me a summer job, if you and dad sign a paper saying it's alright."

"What kind of job?" Her mother asked filling a pot with all of the ingredients.

Ruth told her about becoming a Firewatcher. She emphasized the money and played down any dangers: "two dollars a day, plus keep, for four months. I could make over two hundred fifty dollars this summer and buy us a station wagon to help around the farm."

Helen asked her daughter more questions about being a Firewatcher and Ruth shaded the truth many times.

She also showed her the County consent form and her new driver's license. “All you have to do is sign the waiver and I can be a County Employee.

As the two talked, Helen kept one eye on the kitchen clock. This was Saturday afternoon, payday at the lumber mill where Oscar worked. If he drove straight home from the mill, he would be sober and at the farm within the hour. If he was late and drunk, Ruth’s hopes and dreams could be shattered like a broken glass.

“Your father will never go for this scheme Ruthie. A young girl like you working in the woods alone is just too dangerous. Anyhow, what do you know about camping out in the wilderness?”

“He would agree mom, if you stood up for me. You can teach me how to camp out, how to cook and how to survive in the forest. Please mom, let me have this job as my graduation present,” Ruth said with pleading eyes.

Helen stared back at her daughter with a loving expression. “You’re growing up so fast honey; I don’t know what to do,” she said lifting the stew pot onto the woodstove. “Your father will be home soon. You get your chores done and we’ll see what he has to say.”

It was just like Roy had said: in life, expect the unexpected. Oscar drove his beat up old 1930 Model-A pick-up down the Shangri-La driveway an hour late! Not a good beginning. But, Oscar amazed them all. Not only was he as sober as a preacher, he even brought with him three bags of groceries, ten sacks of desperately needed fertilizer, and a six-pack of cold Rainier Beer. But the biggest surprise of all was the smile on his face. Ruth helped him with the cargo and asked about the windfall. Oscar was a big man, with huge hands, and broad muscular shoulders from manhandling bundles of cedar shingles at work. In his early forties, he still had coal back hair with a sandy complexion and a thin pencil mustache. "I showed them all today Ruthie, we have some celebrating to do."

That evening the family ate in the dining room, something they hadn't done since last Christmas Eve. With a cold beer in hand, and plate full of hot stew, Oscar told them about his amazing day.

The mill had hired two additional Shingle Weavers to help fulfill the contract for the Naval Air Station. There were now six Splitters working for the mill. So the company had a little contest with a twenty dollar prize. Whoever split the most bundles, in a ten hour shift, would become the new shop foreman and be paid three bits a buddle from now on out. Oscar won! He split twenty seven bundles of shakes in ten hours!

"Between my prize money, and my daily output, I made over thirty-five dollars today!" Oscar gloated. "Those five other Weavers just couldn't keep up with me."

Helen and Ruth heard excitement in his voice again. He had some of his confidence back and he continued talking about the contest through dinner and the clean-up. But his news overshadowed Ruth and she had to wait patiently for just the right time. But when it came, Oscar was on his forth bottle of beer. That's when Helen opened a bottle for herself and gave Ruth a quick wink.

"Your daughter has a boy-friend. He's coming to her graduation. She has also been offered a summer job working for the County planting trees," Helen lied with another wink to Ruth. "All we have to do is sign a paper saying its ok with us."

Oscar shook his head with a frown, "How much are they offering to pay?"

"Two dollars a day," Ruth answered proudly. "Plus my keep."

"What keep?" Her father asked with a confused look.

"They will buy her lunch each day she's in the woods," Helen answered quickly.

"No, those cheap bastards at the ounty should be paying more than two lousy dollars a day. If we were in Norway, the socialist government wouldn't allow such a thing."

"Well husband, we don't live in Norway anymore." Helen answered with an alluring smile. "It's getting late, so let's go to bed. We will see how we feel about this job in the morning."

"What the hell do you know about planting trees? Oscar asked Ruth. "You don't know a damn thing about working in the woods."

"I can learn father, just give me a chance."

"No, I'm not signing any papers for the County," Oscar said firmly. "Ruthie can stick around here this summer helping out with the farm."

Helen gave her daughter one last wink with an encouraging nod.

Surprise, surprise, the next morning Helen discreetly showed Ruth the county consent form with both of her parents signature. "How did you manage that mom?" Ruth asked with wide eyes. She smiled back and simply said "My girly ways honey! Someday you'll have these girly ways as well."

With the excuse of installing new curtains at the Hebo Café, Helen used her husband's pick-up truck to drive to town to buy a new curtain rod. She really didn't need the rods, what she needed was the real scoop from the County Forester about this Firewatch business. If he couldn't reassure her about Ruth's safety, Helen would tear up the signed consent form.

She found Chief Jacobson in his third floor cubby hole talking with a volunteer fireman. The young man excused himself from the office as Helen approached with a sour face.

"You must be the man that filled my daughter's head with all that malarkey about being a Firewatcher."

Eric looked at her as he stood up with his hand out, "And you would be?"

"Helen Nelson, my daughter is Ruth Nelson," she replied in a demanding voice. "I need to know a lot more about this so-called summer job before I give you our consent form."

Eric gestured to the empty chair, "Please have a seat Helen, and I'm more than happy to tell you about our Fire Watch program. And yes, I encouraged Ruth to join us. Let me tell you why…"

Using his pictures again, Eric reminded her of the three devastating forest fires of the 1930's. Then he gave her a brief history of the different Firewatch programs used throughout the Oregon Forests. "Our lookouts do more than just watch out for fires, they also report weather conditions and this year they will be a part of the Aircraft Warning System called AWS which was established last year. Our lookouts will report all sightings of aircraft, friend or foe, and radio back their position and direction as they approach our forests. People like Ruth, and our other volunteers, will be our eyes and ears of any approaching dangers from wild fires, storms and/or enemy aircraft."

Chief Forester Eric Jacobson had missed his calling; he should have been a salesman! He was as slick as silk and as knowledgeable as a walking encyclopedia. "Your daughter will play an important role in doing her part for the war effort."

"But will she be safe in the woods all alone?" Helen asked.

"I will be in contact via shortwave radio with all five of my Firewatch lookouts, day or night, until the fire season is over. They will get four days a month off, with pay, and I'll bring the supplies and food to them twice a month. You can visit Ruth anytime, if you don't mind traveling the back roads and log roads of the woods. Think of this as a Tom Sawyer adventure."

Eric opened his desk drawer and handed her two typed written pages of instructions. The first was what personal items she would need living in the towers and another list of what to expect while living in the wilderness. "If the County Commissioners approve her, you can help her out by collecting her personal items and giving her some tips on survival. None of our lookouts have ever had any injuries or deaths working as Firewatchers. This is a safe program." By the time they finished, Helen had a deep respect for the program and Chief Forester. He was a man she could trust. She handed him the signed consent form. "Keep a sharp eye on my Ruthie. She can be bull-headed" "

## Chapter Four

### Once a Mother

Ruth was delighted with her mother's support, but Helen kept reminding her that is was up to the County Commissioners now, so don't get your hopes up. Helen had other things to do as well, like making Ruth a dress for her graduation party. This turned out to be a task of many emotions as Ruth envisioned a simple frock as plain as a gray sky, while Helen demanded a colorful three piece outfit with a neckline and a few bows around her waist. Their negotiations were much like the world at war, with no compromises in sight. This went on for two full days until Oscar demanded a ceasefire or the use of flower sacks as the final dress.

During the day, when Oscar was at work, the girls worked together going over the two pages of instructions. There was warm clothing to gather, shoes and boots to pack away and blankets to be rolled up inside Ruth's down sleeping bag. They bought two canvas water bags, some warm socks and a rain jacket with a hood. Ruth also purchased a notebook so she could write a diary as the days played out. She also borrowed a few books from Lucy Wilson, one of which was a first aid manual as Lucy was thinking about becoming a nurse.

Helen showed Ruth how to make a fire in almost any weather and how to cook over an open flame. And how to search the forest floor for greens and berries that she could eat. Then she learned about hygiene in the woods and how to keep varmints away from her food.

The second list mentioned efficiency with fire arms, so Helen brought out an old 12-gauge shotgun and a .32 caliber pistol and took her daughter target practicing. The weapons were loud and the guns kicked back in their hands and shoulders. Neither one of them could hit the old coffee cans they used as targets. The only damage they did was a few bullet holes in the barn.

"I'll take the guns with me, because they are on the list," Ruth said rubbing her shoulder. "But I won't be using them."

Most of the time, they worked together like hand and glove. Then, with the dress completed, came the Saturday night dance for Ruth's graduation. Because there was only a handful of graduates the commencement ceremony went by quickly with Ruth talking as the class valedictorian about her brother Nick, and all the other men and women, preparing to go off to war. As she was speaking from a raised podium Roy entered the gymnasium all dressed up in his blue and black deputy sheriff uniform. He looked like a movie star from central casting and Ruth had butterflies in her stomach as she finished up with her speech. The audience applause found Roy frozen in place clapping his hands while gazing up at Ruthie. What a marvelous change of appearance: gone were baggy overalls, the rolled up pant legs and high top tennis shoes. All replaced by a figure flattering sky blue dress with a swing skirt and modest scoop neckline and her blond hair rolled up in a soft bun. She even had makeup on, with black pumps and nylon stockings. Like a chameleon, the tomboy had morphed herself into a princess.

After the ceremony, as the room was being prepared for the dance, Ruth introduced Roy to her parents. Oscar did not seem to recognize the deputy from the barroom brawl. Relieved from that worry, he gave Ruth a small wrapped box.

"Here's a little something for your graduation," Roy said with fond eyes. "When in the woods, use it to call for help."

Ruth opened the box and found a silver coach's whistle on a chain, just like the one Roy had in his pocket. "Thank you," Ruth said slipping the chain over her head and gazing at the whistle. "I will use it to stay safe in the woods."

Oscar frowned, "I never used a whistle in woods. That sounds a little silly to me."

Helen jabbed him softly with a smile. "Nice sentiment officer Roy, I'm sure Ruthie will use it often."

Reaching into his pocket Roy gave Ruth an envelope, "I have another gift for you from the county, effective Monday morning you're the newest Tillamook County Employee. I'll pick you up at 8AM and drive you to orientation at the Air Station."

Oscar looked puzzled, "Why the need for an orientation to plant trees? It's simple enough; you plant a sapling in the dirt and it grows. "

With the Glenn Miller Orchestra playing the Chattanooga ChooChoo from a record player, Helen looked at Ruth and Roy, "You kids go dance, I'll explain to Oscar why. High school is over. Your life is before you. Go make some memories."

And what a party they had! Being the valedictorian Ruth and Roy were first on the floor. As they came together for their dance, Roy whispered in her ear, "You are the prettiest of them all."

Ruth blushed turning her face away from Roy. "You're my first dance as a young woman. These will be a medley of memories."

They looked a little awkward at first, but as the evening rolled by their steps found the rhythm of the music and they flowed together like an Arthur Murray couple. That night Roy danced with every girl in the graduating class, including Lucy three times. He was polite and friendly with all the parents and the students. Ruth did the same with all the boys in her class. Memories were made, and for a few short hours the war was forgotten.

On Monday morning Roy pulled up to Shangri-La driving his pick-up truck and opened the passenger door for Ruth with sour look on his face. As she got into the car, Helen came running out of the backdoor with a tin lunch bucket in hand. "Wait, wait I made you kids some lunch."

Ruth was embarrassed, "I'm sure they will feed us mom. I'm not a child anymore."

Helen handed her the bucket, "Once a Mother, always a Mother."

Roy said not a word.

## Chapter Five

### Orientation

The Saturday night shindig for graduation had lasted well past ten in the evening, which was a rare occasion for a room full of farmers. Roy and Ruth had shared the last dance, then said farewell to her classmates and friends. It had been an evening full of memories and unfamiliar feelings for Ruth. There was something special about Roy. Was it love? Infatuation? Or both? Ruth didn't know.

That morning, she found herself in Roy's pick-up, going to work for the first time as a Firewatcher for Tillamook County. Decked out in new blue overalls, her favorite jean jacket, and a red bandana, Ruth sat in the passenger seat next to Roy. He had a long face and angry eyes and hadn't said a word to her all morning.

"Riding with you is like riding with an ice wagon. What's going on?"

"Nothing," he answered sternly. "I just don't like to be lied to."

"What lie?" Ruth asked.

Roy shook his head and glared at her. "How old are you, really?"

"What? Explain that, please."

"After the dance Saturday night, while you were saying good-by to your friends, your father walked me to my car. He was in a surly mood and had a few things to say to me, things like, 'Stay away from my daughter. She's jailbait to you.' Those are his words, not mine."

"What's jailbait?" Ruth demanded, glaring back at him.

"In Oregon, the age of consent is sixteen. Oscar told me you're only fifteen. You lied to me."

"Consent to do what? We didn't do anything wrong. I don't understand."

"Consent to go out with an older man," Roy answered. "If you're only fifteen and I go out with you, I'm not only robbing the cradle, I'm breaking the law. That's not good for a deputy sheriff's reputation or for my family. You told me you were seventeen, not fifteen. I'm no cradle robber, so we can't see each other anymore."

Ruth was dumbfounded. "I was born on the July 20, 1925. I don't have a birth certificate because I was born at home. But I do have my mother's Bible, where she wrote out my name and my date of birth. I'll be eighteen come this July. Would you like to see her Bible?"

Roy looked bewildered. "Then why would your father lie to me about your age? I don't get it. He was mad about it."

Ruth smiled at him. "Think about it, Roy. You're the first adult man in my life. He's just jealous about you hanging around me and dancing with his little girl."

Roy nodded his scowl evaporating. "Alright, I guess that makes sense." He smiled. "But you'll have to show me your mom's Bible when I drive you home, this afternoon."

Ruth smiled back at him, her mind twisting in knots. *One lie always leads to another.*

There were two gigantic blimps tethered to the towers when Roy pulled into the main gate at the Air Station and showed his identification to the guard.

"She's with me," he told the gatekeeper. "Firewatch Orientation."

The young sailor checked a list on his clip-board and gave Roy directions to the headquarters building. "Stay away from the tarmac and in-between the white lines. No picture taking allowed and no stopping along the way."

As they drove under the shadows of the two blimps, Ruth put her head outside the passenger window and looked up at the dirigibles with an amazed smile. "What a sight to see," she yelled back at Roy. "Starting today, I'm part of the war effort."

Roy dropped Ruth off at headquarters. "Duty calls," he said to her. "I'll drive you home after work. I look forward to seeing your mom's Bible."

Ruth nodded, her head still swirling.

In a second floor briefing room of the headquarters building, Chief Forester Jacobs stood by a table with two uniformed sailors. One was a Navy Commander, dressed in a blue uniform with three rows of colorful ribbons on his chest. The commander was tall and handsome, although he was missing his right arm. The other naval officer was Oriental, dressed in the khaki uniform of a Lieutenant JG, with a Navy Medical insignia pinned to his collar. The table in front of the men held half a dozen items, big and small, and three large relief maps of the forests surrounding the Tillamook Valley.

Across from this was another table, where all five of the Firewatch lookouts were sitting together for the first time. They were an unusual looking group: three men and two women of varying ages, dressed in an assortment of working clothes. The lookouts were all ordinary civilians with pencils and notebooks in hand, ready to start work.

"Welcome to the 1942 Firewatch season," Chief Jacobs said, decked out in his firehouse uniform. "Over the next few days, I'm going to brief you on what you should expect." He gestured to the one-armed officer. "This is Commander Cash, our liaison officer. The other gentleman is Lieutenant JG Wong, the flight surgeon for the Air Station. This morning, these two officers will help explain the equipment you'll need in the field and how to use it. If you have any questions during our presentation, just ask."

The lookouts were all stealing glances at Commander Cash's missing arm, and he addressed their silent curiosity. "I was a pilot at Pearl Harbor on December 7th," he told the lookouts with a cold glare. "My wingman and I both made it into the air, but we were shot down by friendly fire. He died. I lived, but without my right arm. It was medical people like Doctor Wong who saved my life on that tragic day. Now I've been put in command of this Air Squadron. I'm the boss of the blimps, while Chief Jacobs is the boss of the fire towers. Our common mission is to protect our forest lands. America needs all the timber we can provide in order to win this war, and we will do our best to protect it for the harvest."

Chief Jacobs opened his briefcase and removed some papers, which he handed around to the lookouts.

"This morning, we'll spend our time getting to know each other, and learning how to use the tools on the table to do our jobs. After the noon meal, the Navy will teach us how to operate the new shortwave radios. And, because we are now part of the Volunteer Aircraft Warning System, the government has also provided us with some much needed additional equipment. Commander Cash and Doctor Wong will help explain and demonstrate each item."

With the wide-eyed lookouts giving the two officers their complete attention, each item on the table was described and passed around the room. The first was a prismatic compass, a small hand instrument that surveyors used to triangulate areas within the forest. "Keep this hand compass with you at all times," Commander Cash told them. "Use it to plot out the directions of any aircraft, fires or smoke you may see."

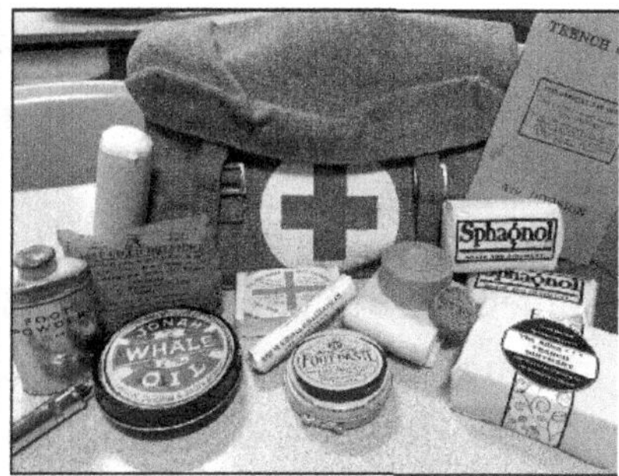


**Prismatic compass & First Aid kit**

The next item was a pair of binoculars with lenses rated at 7X50. Chief Jacobs told them that the field glasses would be used every day in search of aircraft and fires. While passing around the glasses, Chief Jacobs spoke up. "You will notice that all of our equipment is WWI Surplus. With the shortages we have today, thank God for the Navy's frugality. "

Then a First Aid kit was handed around while Doctor Wong talked about its contents. "These kits are older than some of us in this room. Use yours sparingly for beestings, bug bites and sprained ankles. If you have anything more serious, radio me and I'll make a tower call."

The last two items were a flare gun and an all-weather thermometer. Commander Cash commented on these items. "Don't use the flare gun unless you absolutely have to, since the flare itself can cause a forest fire. But if you get trapped in a wildfire, use the flare gun so one of my blimps can locate you and help douse the flames."

"When we move you into the towers on Wednesday," Chief Jacobs said, handing out more papers to the lookouts, "You will find all of these items and your shortwave radio waiting in your nest."

Ruth raised her hand and asked the first question. "What weather information do we need to report each day?"

The chief answered, "Just the temperature, wind direction, and current conditions of visibility, whether it's raining, foggy, or clear."

He moved to the maps and held them up for everyone to see, while Commander Cash passed out books with silhouettes of airplanes and explained the Aircraft Warning System[1] in great detail. "Teach yourselves these silhouettes and tell us the type of aircraft, along with the compass heading and estimated altitude – high, medium or low – of all the aircraft you see in the sky. You are our eyes and ears, so be alert and use the radio to report what you

[1] (AWS)

see."

"What about ships at sea?" one lookout asked.

"Yes," the commander answered. "Ships as well, until we get our new radar system."

"What about fishing boats?" another lookout asked. "They could be smuggling in saboteurs or contraband."

"Yes," Chief Jacobs replied hesitantly, "but let's not go overboard with any spy stuff. Dick Tracy has that espionage stuff under control." The watchers chuckled.

Still standing at the map table he continued. "For now, I'm going to assign each of you to a watchtower location, with your name and radio handle clearly marked on our maps. Tomorrow, we will do a flyover of your assigned towers, to give you a feel for the landscape you'll be responsible for watching. Then, on Wednesday, you will move into your towers and begin your watch."

As the chief passed around a list of the individual names, their radio names, and their tower locations, he told the group, "I had some fun coming up with the radio handles. We will use these names all season, so please don't make any changes." He gestured at his lookouts. "Now, please join me here at the map table, so you can see where your tower is located and how they are all interconnected by logging roads or line of sight."

The lookouts, gathered around the table and started talking with one another as they studied the maps and the contour of the landscape. Ruth wrote down her first notes in her tablet with observations about her fellow lookouts and the towers to which they were assigned: five total strangers who seemed to have little in common.

## Firewatcher Stations & Personnel

**Henry Hoyt**, age 75, retired lighthouse keeper. Radio-name: *Pops*. Six seasons as a Firewatcher. Henry had gray hair, smoked a pipe and had a weathered face. Assigned watch tower: Nestucca Dunes.

**Margaret Smith**, age 62, retired school teacher. Radio-name: *Little Bird*. Three seasons as a Firewatcher. Margaret wore a pair of jeans and a man's wool shirt, with a leather jacket and boots. The only thing missing was her motorcycle. She had an eastern accent and said she was from Brooklyn, New York. Assigned watch tower: Crow's Nest.

**Hank Johnson**, age 21, college student. Radio-name: *Eagle Eye*. First time as a Firewatcher. Young and athletic, Hank had sandy hair and told his draft board he'd be working for a critical wartime government job over the next five months. They approved his release from the draft until the end of the summer. Assigned watch tower: Buzzard Butte.

**Silver Cloud**, age unknown. Half-breed Indian. Radio-name: *Tonto*. First time as a Firewatcher, wears buckskins with a beaded belt and moccasins: a quiet man with olive skin and black eyes. He claims his father was the Chief of the Nestucca Indians. Assigned watch station: Thunder Mountain.

**Ruth Nelson**, age 17. Radio-name: *Cloud Girl*. First time as a Firewatcher. Assigned station: Hebo Butte.

As they finished up with the maps and other items, Chief Jacobs reminded them of their overall duties. "You are always a Firewatcher, first and foremost. Use the Osborne Fire Finder in each of your towers to track and locate any flames or smoke you might see. I will personally show each of you how to work the Fire Finder when we get to your tower. Report all dangerous findings immediately. Once we know where to start looking, we'll contact the other towers to confirm. You are also a weather watcher, so report current weather conditions twice a day. And, finally, you're now a member of the Aircraft Warning System, so study your silhouettes and the different types of enemy aircraft."

After listening to all the duties of her new job, Ruth felt proud to be part of the Firewatch team. While her brother Nick might fight the Japs with bullets, she would remain on the home front, using her own wits and eyes. While Japan had Tokyo Rose, Tillamook County had the 'Cloud Girl.' She was determined to do her best.

After a meal of spam sandwiches and fried potatoes at the Officers Club, the team returned to headquarters to learn how to send and receive shortwave messages on the radio network that the chief had set up. It wasn't complicated, but it required an understanding of the many different frequencies used on shortwave links.

Shortwave radio is a frequency that operates between the FM and AM bands on a standard radio. Shortwave can travel exceptionally long distances, which makes it an excellent option for anyone hoping to reach a wide audience, especially at night. But this type of shortwave equipment required electricity to operate, so car batteries were used as the power source for sending and receiving messages. Freshly recharged batteries were brought to the towers every two weeks, along with other supplies. In the evenings, the lookouts were allowed to talk with each other if they used a hand-cranked battery charger for power. The towers even had a backup communication system of semaphore flags, if all else failed. Nothing was left to chance.

**Shortwave can travel exceptionally long distances, especially during the night.**

Roy returned to pick Ruth up at 5 o'clock. He found her standing outside the headquarters building, talking shop with the other lookouts. They were all excited about what they had learned that day.

"Tomorrow, we're going to ride in a blimp," she told him, getting into his truck. "And yes, I was assigned to your old tower at Hebo Butte. Today, I learned all about shortwave radios and even semaphore flags."

Excited words continued to roll off her lips like machine gun rounds as he turned south on 101 toward her home. Roy heard every detail of the day's happenings, right down to the descriptions she had written about of her fellow lookouts. Ruth talked on and on without stopping until they got to Hebo Junction. Then she asked about his day.

"We are still working the convict crews, making ready all the watch towers for you lookouts on Wednesday. I did see a worrisome sign today, cougar tracks in the dirt around Hebo Butte. That's a very dangerous animal, Ruth. Your mother told me at the dance that you weren't very skilled with a pistol, and that's not good when it comes to cougars."

Ruth reached inside one of her pockets and brought out her silver whistle. "I have this, your gift. I'll whistle away any cougar that comes across my path."

Roy frowned at her. "This isn't the Wizard of Oz and you're not Dorothy! When I get you home, I'll give you a shooting lesson, after I see your mother's Bible."

Ruth gave him a puzzled look. "Oh yes, the Bible. I almost forgot."

Pulling into Shangri-La, Roy parked his truck next to the barn. Oscar was still not home from work and Helen was nowhere to be found. Ruth went into the house and moments later came back outside with an old Bible in hand.

She handed it to Roy. "First page."

He opened it to the first page and found what appeared to be the names for Nick and Ruth. The only problem was the dates of birth as the entire Bible, had been written in Norwegian. There was one circled date written in English next to Ruth's name: July 20, 1925. Roy was lost, as he couldn't read another word on the front page cover.

"What's it all say?" he asked Ruth.

She pointed to the words, "This is for Nick and this is for me. *Tusen ni hundre og tjue-sju* in Norwegian means July 20, 1925. That makes me seventeen years old, just like I said."

Roy shook his head with a grin. "That's good enough for me, Ruthie. Go get your gun and let's do some shooting."

As Ruth returned to house with the Bible, she was pleased that Roy hadn't noticed the different colored ink she had used to forge the circled date of July 20th 19*28.* Using a Bible for another one of her little white lies didn't sit well with her. But who would ever really know?

# Chapter Six

**Up, up & away!**

Early the next morning, the lookout crew met again at the briefing room of the headquarters building. This time, however, two of the lookouts told Chief Jacobs and Commander Cash that they wanted nothing to do with a fly-over, riding inside a blimp.

"I remember watching the newsreels when the Hindenburg exploded in 1937," Henry Hoyt said, shaking his head. "I want nothing to with these Zeppelins. They are too dangerous for this old man."

"I agree," Margaret Smith added. "I've never flown before and I don't want to start now."

Commander Cash smiled at the dissenters. "That's not a problem. We have a lot of white-knuckle flyers here at the Air Station. But you should know a few facts first. The Hindenburg used hydrogen gas to make it lighter than air, while we use helium to do the same. Hydrogen is highly combustible and one small spark can make it explode. Helium is not combustible at all and can fly through a lightning storm without any problems. Stay on the ground if you wish or come fly with us like a bird."

“The Thunderbird is the God of our Gods, and I ride on his back many times,” Silver Cloud said with a stone face. “Now I ride on whales back with no fear. Whales are also one of our Gods.”

“How long would we be up in the air?” Henry asked.

“A couple hours for the flyover of the forests and three more hours for our regular mission up the north coast to the Columbia River and back.”

“Will you fly by the lighthouses?”

“Yes, all three of them,” the commander answered.

Henry nodded. “If that’s case, you can count me in. I’ve always wondered what the lighthouses looked like from a bird's perspective.”

With his agreement to fly, even Margaret changed her mind. “If I’m going to die flying, I guess today is as good a time as any.”

**Before and during World War II, 134 K-class blimps were built and configured for patrol and anti-submarine warfare operations. They were extensively used by the US Navy over the Atlantic and Pacific Oceans.**

With the fear of flying overcome, Commander Cash told the lookouts his flight plan for the flyovers of the many different forests. The blimp would have a flight crew of five airmen, consisting of a pilot, copilot, navigator, and two riggers who were also forward and aft gunners. The airship would climb to two thousand feet over the ocean and fly south down the coastline. Then it would turn east at Nestucca Bay and climb to five thousand feet and fly over the mountainous forests.

"Keep your eyes out for log roads, lakes, and trails as possible escape routes in case you get trapped in a forest fire," The chief said. "Getting out of the woods safely after reporting a fire should always be Job One."

"How fast can a blimp fly?" Ruth asked.

"Our cruising speed is about 60 mph," the commander answered. "And we have a range of over 2,200 miles."

"How many blimps fly out of the Air-Station?"

"Right now? Just two," Cash answered. "We have four more coming, in the next few months. And one more thing before we go to the flight line," he continued, "We will be sitting in the back of the gondola, behind the flight crew. If you have questions, ask me or Chief Jacobs. Don't disturb the flight crew. Oh yes, and go to the bathroom now. There's only a honey-bucket for a latrine on the blimp."

A crew of sailors held the ship in place with ropes and lines, and fitting a dozen people inside the gondola of a blimp was like adding another sardine to a can. The fit was tight. Finally, with everyone aboard, the Pratt & Whitney motors warmed up as more helium was pumped into the bladder of the dirigible. Slowly, ever so slowly, the blimp started to rise and was released from the tie-down tower.

Then the motors engaged. As the tarmac got smaller, the ship was finally airborne, and the fire crews breathed a sigh of relief. That was when Ruth noticed that Henry and Margaret were holding hands. The two white-knuckle fliers were comforting each other. How sweet was that?

At two thousand feet, the flight down the coast was spectacular. Thanks to the large windows of the gondola, there wasn't a bad seat in the airship. It was as if you could reach out and touch the rugged coastline. The teal green of the pounding surf and the midnight blue of the clear sky merged together like a painting in a museum, Mother Nature's brushstrokes at her best. The ride inside the gondola was surprisingly quiet, with only a buzzing sound and a slight vibration from the electric motors. The ride was as smooth as silk.

At Nestucca Bay, the blimp turned inland. Along the shore of the bay, they could see the fifty-foot watch tower of Nestucca Dunes, giving the fire lookout Henry Hoyt excellent views of the forests farther south, and north to the Tillamook Valley. He also had views of the shipping lanes and east to Mt. Hebo. The Nestucca Dunes tower was like an anchor for all the forests on the western slopes of the Coastal Mountains.

As the blimp turned inland and gained altitude, they flew right over Shangri-La. Ruth could see her house, the barn, and the cultivated fields. Everything seemed tiny. There was something exhilarating about flying, and Ruth couldn't take her eyes off the landscape.

A few minutes later, she could see the forty-foot tower of Hebo Butte atop Mt. Hebo. It looked charming and peaceful from the air. She could see the access road from County Road 22 crossing a few streams and leading up the mountain to her tower. She also noticed another road surrounding a nearby lake. The two roads reminded her to bring Nick's bicycle when she moved in, the next day. Having her bike would give her added mobility.

The chief turned to her from his seat. "On clear days, Hebo Butte has a direct view of the Nestucca Dunes. And you'll have a good view of the Crow's Nest, on the western slopes. What do you think?"

"I'm ready to move in!" she answered with excitement, her gaze glued to the window.

They visited all five towers that morning, and each lookout got a bird's-eye view of where they would be working for the next five months. Chief Jacobs gave them a few tips on what to watch out for, around each tower. "Keep an eye out for lakes, streams, and ponds. Always have two escape routes in the back of your head. Stay near the water whenever possible."

Just before noon the blimp turned for the open sea again and plotted a course up the coastline to the Columbia River. For this part of the mission, the flight crew turned serious, watching out for any enemy ships or shadows of submarines lurking under the water. Flying at an altitude of two thousand feet, they soon passed the Tillamook Air Station and continued on with their search.

About this time, the navigator handed out sack lunches with warm bottles of Coca-Cola. "Spam sandwiches again," he said with a frown. "You'd think, just once, we could have hotdogs."

Later, they flew right over the Tillamook Rock Lighthouse, with its beacon blinking and its foghorns blasting. Tilly stood as the only operational lighthouse still working on the Pacific coastline, because of the war. With the blimp horns sounding a salute, the ship continued up the coast to the town of Seaside, Oregon. On this warm spring day, the beaches were busy and people waved at the blimp as it flew by. The crew and the lookouts returned the gestures.

**Seaside Oregon 1942** © Seaside Museum

At the south jetty at Point Adams, the blimp crossed the Columbia River, where two new Liberty Ships were heading out to sea. Those ships were the vanguard of a massive fleet being built up-river in the shipyards of the Pacific Northwest. In the coming years, hundreds more ships just like them would cross the Bar on their way to the battlefields of the Pacific. America was just awaking, and the world would soon feel her power and might as she built the largest naval Armada in the history of mankind.

The blimp circled the North Head Lighthouse and Cape Disappointment and then turned for home. That was when the lookouts noticed a new type of ship docked at the Astoria pier. Commander Cash referred to the new ship as a Casablanca-class Aircraft Carrier. "We will have fifty of those new ships in the next two years," he said proudly to the lookouts. "The Japs will soon get what they have coming, and I'll have a little revenge for my missing arm."

All the lookouts nodded their agreement with hate in their eyes. The Japanese were thoroughly despised for their sneak attack on Pearl Harbor, and their day of infamy was coming.

Upon returning to the Air Station, the flight crew made a near-perfect landing, and the blimp was soon tied to her tethering tower. As the lookouts departed the gondola, they were all buzzing about their day in the blimp. It was an experience they would cherish for the rest of their years.

"Tomorrow is moving day," Chief Jacobs reminded them as they walked across the tarmac. "Firehouse at 8AM. Check and double-check your personal belongings. It's going to be a long day and your first night at camp."

**Casablanca-class Aircraft Carriers**

**Liberty Ships on the Move**

## Chapter Seven

**The Nest**

The next morning, while Ruth said good-by to her mother and loaded her duffle bag into her father's truck, Oscar lifted a wicker laundry basket filled with food stuffs into the back.

"You phone me when you get situated," Helen pleaded, hugging her daughter.

"There are no phones in our towers, Mom, just radios connected to the firehouse and the Air Station. They will always know what's going on. I'll send you letters whenever I can."

Helen sounded forlorn as she said, "You're going to be all alone out there, honey, I'll pray for you every night."

Ruth picked up her dog. "I'll always have Winnie, my companion and watch dog."

Lifting the bicycle into his truck, Oscar laughed, "Good luck with that notion. Your dog is as dumb as a fence post."

Ruth put her hands over the dog's ears. "Don't say that Father. You'll hurt his feelings!"

"That mutt has no feelings. Well, we better get going, if we're going to get there on time."

With the truck loaded, and Winnie settled next to Ruth in the cab, Oscar drove to town and the firehouse. It was moving day.

Oscar had volunteered to take her to the firehouse because there were a few parting words he wanted to say to her. “I want you to stay away from that deputy sheriff you brought to the dance. He’s too old for you.”

“If I was a squaw, I’d have a lodge full of papooses by now,” Ruth answered with a grin. “Besides, the deputy is just my friend. What did he ever do to you?”

Oscar frowned at her. “You’re not a damn squaw so don’t sass me back. I don’t like him or his father. They both are sucking on the hind tit of the government.”

“That’s a bum rap, Father. The sheriff works for the voters, while Roy works for the county. He and Chief Jacobs will watch out for me, this summer. And when the season is over, with my earnings, we can buy a used pickup, something we need around the farm.”

“I still don’t like him. He’s just sniffing around the jailbait,” Oscar said.

“Please, Father, don’t ever call me that again. It’s condescending.”

“Don’t use your two-bit words with me! He’s just a horny toad, like all men, which leads to unwed mothers with families no one wants.”

“Do you mean like Nick?” Ruth asked. “In Mom’s Bible, his date of birth and your wedding date are only a few months apart. Were you a horny toad, Dad?

Shaking his head, Oscar replied, “That’s none of your damn business.”

“Well then,” Ruth replied, “Roy and I should be none of your damn business, as well.”

Oscar glared at his daughter, “Always with your nose in air. You have a lot to learn, little girl. Life isn’t always fair."

Her father was red-faced mad. Had she crossed the line? Gathering her courage, she said, "I do have a favor to ask. Please stop preaching about Norwegian socialism. Nobody in America cares. There's a World War going on now."

The rest of the ride to town seemed endless, with many spirited words exchanged that would soon be regretted. "Don't be such a willful woman," her father finally concluded. "I can still put you over my knee."

"That is true, Father, but you'd have to catch me first, and I can run faster than you."

At the Firehouse, Ruth learned that Roy was taking three of the lookouts to their watch towers: Henry Hoyt, Silver Cloud, and Ruth. Chief Jacobs was doing the same with Margaret Smith and Hank Johnson. "The watch towers are about twenty miles apart from each other, so it will take us most of the day to get you on sight and operational," He had said to his lookouts. "All right, let's get loaded up and on the road."

Oscar pulled his truck into the driveway next to Roy's Studebaker, still fuming from his conversation with Ruth. He helped transfer her cargo to Roy's truck without saying a word but, when he was done, Oscar walked over and confronted Roy in front of everyone.

"I've got my eyes on you, deputy," he yelled pointing at Roy. "Keep your horny toad hands off my daughter. If you don't, I'll put a shotgun up your ass and pull the trigger."

Everyone on the driveway seemed stunned. The

two men glared at each other like a pair of bulls in a ring. Then Roy, with his fists clenched, shook his head. “That won’t be necessary, Oscar. Ruth and I are only friends. More than likely, I won’t even see her again until the end of the fire season.”

Oscar’s look of anger drained from his face. After a moment, he turned for his truck and climbed into the cab. Rolling down his window, he started the motor and shouted to Ruth, “I’m your father, little girl. I will always watch out for you. Go save the damn forest and get paid the two lousy dollars a day from this penny-pinching county.”

*How embarrassing was that!* Ruth thought to herself, watching her father drive away in a cloud of dust. Why did he have to be such a dark cloud in her life?

Roy approached her with a serious expression. “You and Winnie can ride in the back of the truck with Silver Cloud. We’re going to Hebo Butte first. Where’s your whistle?”

Ruth looked at him sadly. “I’m so sorry about what Oscar said.”

“Don’t worry about it, Ruthie. He’s just jealous of his little girl.” Roy said and helped her and Winnie into the back of the truck. “Now put your whistle on and leave it on. We’re going into the wilds of the woods.”

Ruth’s tower, Hebo Butte, was near the summit of Hebo Mountain, some twenty miles from Hebo Junction as the crow flew, and closer to thirty miles away of driving, thanks to the many switchback roads. After the county road, they crossed two small rivers on log bridges, making the journey up the mountain road bumpy and treacherous.

With Winnie in her arms, Ruth rode beside Silver

Cloud, enjoying the rugged beauty of the forest. The canopy of tall fir trees almost blocked out the sky. The forest floor was covered with the yellow-gold of new growth and tall ferns. At almost every turn of the logger's road, creeks and streams flowed off the mountainside and raced to the rivers below. It was cool and damp under the canopy, and the forest seemed filled with every type of bird and small, furry animal, all scurrying into their hiding places. The landscape was overpowering, and Ruth did her best to forget the embarrassment caused by her father.

Silver Cloud seemed to sense her embarrassment. "It is hard for warrior parent to watch young squaw's spirit mission into the forest. They worry about the trails you select. But they will come around to your spirits by the next tribal council."

Ruth thanked Silver Cloud for his encouraging words; it was the most they had said to one another. Silver Cloud, with his stone face, was a quiet man of Indian wisdom.

Close to an hour later, the truck bounced into a natural clearing on top of a rocky butte. There stood the forty-foot-tall Hebo Butte tower. It was an impressive sight, built with unlimited forest views to the north and south. Constructed atop of treated log poles, just like telephone poles, the tower had three levels of steep steps leading up to the small, tin roofed hut that rested on a wooden platform. The spire was like a monolith, overshadowing the wilderness and reminding Ruth of her childhood tree houses.

Roy parked close to the tower and got out of his truck, smiling broadly. "It's just like I remember it from four years ago," he said, looking up at the structure. "It was on this very same date in 1938 that I moved into this nest."

Roy searched through the supplies in the truck and came up with three empty water bags made of canvas and rubber. Turning, he handed the bladders to Henry Hoyt. "You guys take the dog and these water bags down to the lake and fill them up," he requested, pointing to the trailhead across the way, "While Ruth and I do a walk-around of her new home."

With the two lookouts gone, Roy started circling the tower, pointing out details and telling Ruth the good and the bad of living at Hebo Butte. He started at the storage shed/outhouse and explained that it was built of logs and cement, with chinked walls, heavy timbered door, and an inside iron latch. "This outhouse and storage shed is your safe house, if you need it. The door is bear-proof."

On the other side of tower was a root cellar dug into the ground and made with the same construction methods as the storeroom. It, too, was bear-proof. Under the tower itself and, out of the weather, was a cord or more of chopped firewood.

"The convict crew was up here a few weeks ago, clearing the underbrush, opening the trails, and chopping your firewood. Once this supply is gone, you'll have to chop your own. The lake is just about a mile away, for your drinking water and bathing. Keep your dog close when you move down that trail. The big animals always have the right of way."

They climbed the three flights of steps, and Roy showed her how the top flight could be pulled up, like a castle bridge over a moat. He said it helped keep the little critters – squirrels, mice, and rats – out of the nest.

Ruth shivered at the thought of those little 'critters.' She hated rodents, especially rats.

The nest itself was quite small, only a single room of about 300 square feet. There were windows in three of the four walls of the hut, with an outside catwalk and wooden shutters that could be closed if needed. In the center of the little room was the Fire-Finder, an instrument used by fire lookouts for directional bearings to pinpoint smoke and flames.

**Using the Fire Finder was basic mathematics**

Roy gave Ruth her first lesson in using the Fire Finder. It was quite simple, just basic mathematics. Ruth took to the instrument right away. Other than that, the room had a black-iron wood stove, a small table, two folding webbed chairs, and a raised mattress on a wooden platform where Ruth would sleep. Under the windows were shelves and a few bookcases, along with a shiny new shortwave radio of the sort they had just been trained to operate. Roy told her that the Navy had set up the equipment a few days before. On the floor next to the radio were the pair of six-volt car batteries needed to power the radio.

And that was it, Ruth's cocoon for the next few months!

With the noisy return of the other firewatchers from the lake, Roy stepped out onto the catwalk and looked down at them. "I'm going to drop down a basket for the water bags," he shouted. "Then I'll crank them up, using my pulley system. You won't have to use the stairway." Moving back inside the hut, he removed a large 5'x 3' wire basket from where it hung in the rafters. Returning to the catwalk, he fastened the basket to his pulley system and used a rope connected to the basket to hand-crank it down to ground level. "Put the water in the basket along with Ruth's duffle bag and I'll crank it all up."

"What about her dog?" Henry shouted back. "The mutt's stubby legs can't get up those tall steps."

"Put him in the basket, too. He can ride up."

With Ruth watching, Roy carefully cranked up the basket and the dog. "You'll have to do this every time he needs to go outside. Should we just leave him down on the ground level to forage for himself?"

"No!" Ruth answered with a frown. "He's staying with me. I'll crank him up and down."

After one more load in the basket, all of Ruth's belongings and supplies were safely in her hut. With everything scattered about, the little room it looked lived in, and just in time, as it started to rain. Ruth lit a fire in the wood stove to take the chill off.

"All you need now are curtains for the windows," Roy said with a smile. "You will find the blackout curtains in the storeroom."

With both Henry and Silver Cloud anxious to see their towers, Ruth walked Roy to his truck to say goodbye. “Crank up some more firewood,” he suggested "According to the weatherman, you’re going to need it in the next few days. And use the radio if you see or need anything.”

“So I won’t see you again all summer?” Ruth asked sadly as he got into his truck.

He smiled at her. “I’ll stop by, every now and then. Maybe I’ll even bring you a milkshake and a hamburger from the Hebo Café.” He started his Studebaker and winked at her, then added, through the open window.

“Keep that whistle around your neck, and use it if you get into trouble.”

**Interior View of Lookout Tower**

**Hebo Butte Lookout Tower**

# Chapter Eight

## The Neighborhood

With thunder in the sky and rain rolling down her cheeks, Ruth watched Roy's truck disappear down the mountain road. On this, the first day of the fire season, it was raining… and two important men in her life had driven away from her. Was that a bad omen or just a warning of things that might be? For now, she was totally alone, dependent on her own wits.

Wiping the rain off her face, she began by cranking up a load of fire wood, then put on a pot of coffee. As she waited for it to brew, she and Winnie walked around the nest, looking for little surprises left behind by other lookouts over the years.

She found a few books and old magazines stuffed in the shelves. Next to the stove, there were several pieces of flatware, along with pots, pans, and some tin plates. Hanging from the rafters were two hurricane lamps, with a jug of kerosene. In one corner of the room, hidden behind a stack of books, she found a full pint of whiskey and two cans of snuff.

Ruth returned the booze and tobacco to their hiding place without sampling any of the stash. She planned to do that later. She even found an old pair of opera glasses and a map stuffed, into one of the cubby holes. At 4X, they were low-powered, but better than the naked eye.

With the rain still dancing on the tin roof, she poured herself a cup of coffee and sat down in one of the folding chairs to read the manual for the radio equipment. Her instructions were to radio the Air Station and firehouse at 6 o'clock each evening and 9 o'clock each morning. She checked the pocket watch her mother had given her for graduation. That was four hours away and she was tired. She still had much more to do, but it had been a long day, with her emotions bouncing up and down like yo-yo. With her nest warming up with the stove, Ruth soon nodded off.

The sound of a car horn woke her from her nap. She slowly opened her eyes wondering where in the hell she was. But when Winnie started barking, it all came rushing back to her. She was in her hut. It had stopped raining and her fire was smoldering.

As she floundered to her feet, the car horn honked again. She rushed out the door and onto the cat-walk. Looking down from her perch, she spotted Roy standing next to his Studebaker, smoking a cigarette and honking his horn.

"I forgot to give you something," he yelled up. "Can you come down?"

"On my way," she called back, and headed for the stairs with Winnie in her arms.

When she reached Roy's truck, she let Winnie go. "What's all the fuss about?" she asked. "Did you get Henry and Tonto deployed?"

"Yes, they are in their nests," Roy answered, and blew smoke from his mouth. "Have you checked in yet?"

Ruth looked at her watch. “Not yet. I fell asleep, reading the radio manual. But I still have twenty minutes.”

“Good.” Roy opened the door to his truck and rummaged inside. He soon brought out a scabbard knife and handed it to Ruth. “I forgot to give this to you, this morning. You’ll need a good hunting knife, and this blade will help you dress out any game you might kill.”

Ruth grinned at him. “You came all the way back up here to give me this knife?”

Roy moved slowly towards her, stepping on his cigarette butt. He looked at her with a strange smile on his face. “Yes, I did,” he replied, coming even closer. Ruth felt frozen in place. Then he placed both of his hands on her face and gently kissed her on her lips. “And I wanted to steal a kiss from you, for all my good efforts.”

Ruth was speechless for the longest moment, just gazing up at him. Then, blushing, she finally replied, “I think I better radio in. Thank you for the knife.”

Roy got into his truck and started the engine, still with that special look in his eyes. “I like doing nice things for you, Ruth. Keep that whistle and the knife close by.”

In one fluid motion, Ruth leaned in through his open window and kissed Roy back, soft and long. “I like you doing nice things for me, Roy. Come back soon and teach me more.”

*Wow*, was all she could think, running up the stairs to check in on the radio. Her diary would be full of entries tonight. When she had kissed Roy, she had felt the tip of his tongue on her lips. What was that all about?

The spring weather on the north coast of Oregon was always a crap-shoot. One moment, it would be sunny and warm. The next moment, a deluge of rain could fall, with the sun still shining. Between those two extremes came what the locals called 'sticky rain,' a dampness that followed a person around like morning dew. So it was for Ruth, the first few days at Hebo Butte.

Her first night in the tower was long and unfamiliar, filled with all the forest sounds of animals, wind, and rain. The next morning, she visited the outhouse for the first time. It was an exploration she had feared, all night. Not knowing what might be hiding inside the little log structure, she approached it with the whistle in her lips and a flashlight in her hand. She opened the heavy wood door, expecting to face something that crawled, bit, or clawed.

But, with the door wide open, she found nothing but a one-hole privy with a wooden toilet seat. The smell inside was nauseating, and she quickly used the facility while taking anxious note of the darkness of the little room and its inside iron door-latch. The outhouse/shed was indeed animal proof.

Afterward, she explored the storeroom, paying careful attention to what supplies, tools, and other items were on hand. The room was stocked with camping equipment, canned foods, and dry goods. Finding blackout curtains, lengths of rope, signaling flags, and a mirror, she moved these items to her nest. Here, for the first time since arriving at Hebo Butte, she looked at herself in a mirror. Her hair was a mess. Her face was grimy and her overalls dirty. *How could Roy want to kiss such a creature?*

With promising weather, Ruth and Winnie walked to the lake to clean up, that very afternoon. She also had in hand the three empty water bags that needed refilling. Using a tree limb as a walking stick, she found the trail easy and the landscape breathtaking.

As they approached the pond, Ruth got her first look at the lake. It was long and narrow, with a logged-out clearing around the shoreline which made the lake appear bigger than it was. On the water, she could see ducks and geese feeding on the reeds, and a few fish were jumping. Lake Hebo looked like a great resource for fresh game and fish, so she promised herself to bring her fishing pole on her next trip to the pond.

While walking the water's edge, Ruth noticed a pile of dried-up underbrush on the shore. Investigating this mound, she found a small rowboat, upside down, tucked away under the twigs. Turning the dinghy over, she spotted two oars underneath it. The twelve-foot craft looked water tight, so she pushed it out into the shallows of the lake, watching for leaks.

When she found none, she put Winnie in the boat and climbed in herself. Now they could row around the lake. But who owned the boat? She scanned the water and shouted, "Anybody out here?" Only her echo replied. She even blew her whistle a few times, but there was no response. Seeing no other signs of life, she took her clothes off, down to her underwear, and got into the lake, where she washed her body and hair with a bar of soap.

The water was cold, and she kept a cautious eye out. Could there be some voyeur hiding in the bushes? Just then, something swam between her legs. A water snake?

She jumped back into the boat with a shriek, and then realized that it had only been a fish. Still, enough was enough. Her bath was over.

After catching her startled breath, Ruth paddled the boat to shore and dried out her damp clothes in the sun. Then she returned the boat to its upside-down position, under the same pile of twigs. She wanted to keep the craft for herself.

As she and Winnie walked back to the tower that afternoon they were confronted by their first contact with a wild animal. It was a young cougar, perched on a log stump, ready to leap. Ruth didn't panic. Instead, she blew her whistle with a lungful of air, using her walking stick to keep Winnie away from the cat. Wide-eyed, hissing at the dog, the animal at first held its ground but a second blast of the whistle sent it scurrying back into the forest. The only damage done was to Winnie's pride.

Ruth's days soon became regimented. She spent her early mornings scanning the forests for smoke or flames and searching the sky for any aircraft, her binoculars in hand. At 9AM., all five of the lookouts checked in with the Fire Station and the Air Station. Their reports were short: current weather conditions, forest observations, and any aircraft to report. Each report was kept to about two minutes, to help conserve the batteries needed for the radio.

The lookouts used their radio names, and all the others could hear their reports. *Pops* at Nestucca Dunes seemed the busiest, as he also reported passing ships and even fishing boats. *Tonto* at Thunder Mountain gave the shortest reports with the fewest words: "Nothing here."

*Cloud Girl* at Hebo Butte reported seeing smoke three times in the first week but that 'smoke' turned out to be just fog and low clouds, so no action was taken. *Little Bird* at Crow's Nest reported seeing fire and smoke twice in the first week. Both fires were later learned to be authorized slash burns by a local logging company. The first real forest fire, reported by *Eagle Eye* at Buzzard Butte, came on the third day of the season and was doused quickly by the Tillamook Fire Station. During the entire first week, only eight aircraft were reported in the sky. All seemed quiet on the fire-watch front.

After the morning check-ins, Ruth used her bicycle to explore the log roads and trails, looking for high ground that might expand her views of the surrounding forests. With Winnie in the basket, she found some beautiful waterfalls, ponds and creeks, each one whittled out of stone and trees by the hand of God Himself. The Hebo woods offered surprising views with each turn of the road or walk down a trail.

On Ruth's second trip to the lake, she made another discovery close to where she had found the boat. It looked like a pile of junk covered over with a rotting canvas tarp and some tree limbs. Beneath this cover, she found some old metal pots and pans, and several wooden paddles. From the debris, she took away a metal pot to be used as a bedpan. The cache seemed like a mysterious discovery to Ruth, since Chief Jacobs had told the lookouts that all the forests were closed to the general public because of the war.

Weather permitting, when Ruth looked north, she could see Margaret's Crow's Nest tower just above the treetops, some twenty-five miles away. Turning south, she had the same glimpse of Henry's Nestucca Dunes tower. Using the map she had found when she moved in, Ruth calculated that she could see almost sixty miles of forest on a clear day.

**Coffee and Binoculars, the Catwalk Dance**

# Chapter Nine

## Life in the Cloud

By the end of the first week Ruth had come to grips with living in the clouds. The nest she called home was small and compact, but provided her with a roof over her head and the means to cook and care for herself and Winnie. She had discovered, however, that on windy days the tower noticeably swayed as if imitating the tall trees swaying in the forest. It was concerning to her at first, but soon she convinced herself that it was just Mother Nature rocking her cradle.

Cooking was the real challenge in those first few weeks. The small top of the wood stove was all she had to prepare and cook her needs. The laundry basket her mother had sent helped immensely, with mason jars filled with vegetables and fruits. Helen had also sent four dozen corn biscuits, five pounds of beef jerky, and three slabs of bacon, as well as two sacks of beans. Certainly Ruth would not starve on this basic menu, but she missed the fresh meat, eggs, and milk of living on a farm. Ruth had a sweet tooth, as well, and long gone were her mother's pies, cinnamon rolls, and cookies. But she would not complain, to herself or others, about her trivial hardships when so many young soldiers were facing death in the far-off lands of the Pacific.

After her evening meal and her radio check-in, Ruth would traverse the catwalk, binoculars in hand, making one final scrutiny of the forest in the remains of the day. It was from those sunsets that she watched the evening stars come to life and heard the sounds of the creatures in the forest as they started their evening serenade. It was a time of reflection and prayer for her brother Nick, her family, and Deputy Roy. The deputy was on her mind almost every day; she could not escape her infatuation with him.

On clear nights, she often watched *Little Bird* at the Crow's Nest light her hurricane lamps. If she turned west, she could do the same with *Pops* at Nestucca Dunes. Those far-away events always reminded Ruth to do the same with her lamps. As she gazed at their towers through the lenses of her binoculars, she often said out loud, "What are you thinking about, tonight?"

With nightfall, it was time for the radio, powered by the hand-crank generator she used to conserve the batteries. It was Ruth's only entertainment, each and every night. She had taught herself the shortwave frequencies used to hear such people as Tokyo Rose, President Roosevelt's Fireside Chats, and Winston Churchill on the BBC. It took a steady hand, patience, and a strong arm to crank out the electricity needed for the programs. But solitude stalked her, and the radio and her books were all the human contact she had with the outside world. To her own surprise, Ruth was beginning to feel lonely, missing her family and friends. The only other living being she had was Winnie, and she talked to him endlessly.

The war news Ruth learned from the radio was

mostly discouraging. It seemed as though the Japanese were out to conquer the world and, according to Tokyo Rose, they were doing so at full speed ahead. When Ruth wrote notes home, she took care always to fill them with encouraging words about her life and what she was doing to help save the forests. No mention was made about the war or Deputy Roy. She handed off her letters to Chief Jacobs, so that he could hand deliver them to her mother on his next resupply date.

That first resupply date came on the morning of Monday June 15, and Ruth was thrilled to hear the chief's truck pull up next to her tower. Finally she had another person to talk with. Their first order of business was coffee and gossip about the war, the county, the other lookouts, and home. The conversation lasted through a second cup of coffee and a list of all the supplies he had brought with him in his truck: fresh batteries for the radio, more kerosene for the lamps, cans of fruit and vegetables, and two tins of spam, along with one can of corned beef. The meat was most welcome.

"You don't know how hard it is to get canned meats, these days," The chief said with a frown. "The cooks at the Air Station put together the food packages for all my lookouts, and your mother packed another laundry basket especially for you."

Another item on the list caught Ruth's eye. "What is a 'field tub and sink'?" she asked, reading the list.

The chief smiled at her. "You're going to love it. It's a fold-up bathtub and small sink made of rubber and wood. You can fill it up with hot water to take a proper bath or wash your hair."

Ruth chuckled. "Don't tell me the animals are complaining about my smell!"

"Let's just say your nest is a little ripe," Chief Jacobs replied with a grin.

The last item on his list was a notation: June 1$^{st}$ through the 15$^{th}$ payroll due: $32.00.

Ruth thought about her first payday and wondered what to do with it. She had no use for money in the towers. "I have some letters for my mother," she said to him. "So please just give her my letters and my pay. She'll know what to do with it."

Chief Jacobs reached for his briefcase, opened it, and handed Ruth a stack of letters. "These are from your mom." He looked inside his case again and handed her three more envelopes. "Two from Deputy Roy and one from *Little Bird,* across the way at the Crow's Nest. She wants to get to know you better."

Ruth was pleased with all her letters, something to read on the lonely nights. But she was disappointed that Roy had only sent two letters. She'd had hoped for more. His promise to come back for a visit was still ringing in her ears. She felt like Roy had forgotten her. But she said nothing of this to the chief, since it was none of his affair. "Thank you, Chief Jacobs, for being my postman. It's nice to get mail."

"Do you have any mail for Deputy Roy?" He asked.

"No," Ruth blushed. "I've been so busy learning the tower life, maybe next time."

The chief frowned, "He'll be disappointed, he talks of you often."

After the gabfest in the hut, they unloaded the truck,

placing some of the supplies in the root cellar while other goods and the mason jars were hand-cranked up to the nest. Once they had sorted out the supplies, Ruth took a look at the field tub and sink. The tub looked complicated to put together, and it wouldn't be easy to get so much hot water from her tiny stove. With a shrug, she put the tub in the storeroom and kept the little sink for her nest.

While they worked, Ruth told him about finding the boat on the lake, and about the other rubble she had discovered nearby. "I think it's just fishermen or hunters," Ruth told him.

"Well, if it is, they are breaking a Federal Law," he answered. "Without a special permit, these forests are closed for the duration of the war. When we're finished here, let's go have look-see at your discovery."

Once at the lake, they concluded that long-ago poachers and bootleggers had been the source of Ruth's find. She and the chief used the boat to row around the entire lake, looking for fresh signs of people, but found nothing except for a few burned-out camp sites. Chief Jacobs even looked at the rubble Ruth had found. He recognized it as a dismantled still, the kind used by bootleggers during the Prohibition years.

"Back then, the forests were crawling with moon-shiners and gangsters. This would have been a dangerous place to be."

"So you don't think there are any fishermen or hunters up here in the mountains?"

He shook his head, "Other than the row boat, everything I've seen is old and rotting away. That's a good sign. We don't want Hebo Butte compromised by outsiders.

With the whistle around her neck, they walked the trail back towards Hebo Butte. She carried two heavy bags of water, while the chief did the same with two more bags and his pistol on his belt.

"What about me?" Ruth asked. "Can I legally fish and hunt Hebo Lake?"

"Yes. All my lookouts can live off the land, if needed. It's part of our contract with the Federal Government. It's called survival rights."

Returning to the tower, they had lunch together. Then Chief Jacobs moved on. His next supply drop was *Pops* at Nestucca Dunes. It would be late in the evening before he could finish up with *Tonto* on Thunder Mountain.

**The Forest Evening Serenade**

# Chapter Ten

## Smoke & Fire

With the departure of Chief Jacobs, the first thing Ruth did was roam her catwalk with the binoculars to her eyes. After an all-clear scrutiny, she gathered up her letters and sat cross-legged on her sleeping bag, reading the contents out loud to Winnie.

Her mother's words were warm, filled with news and love. As a result of Oscar's new promotion to Foreman, they had hired a twelve-year-old neighbor boy to take on the farm chores while Ruth was away, saving the forest. Helen was taking on other jobs, as well. She helped out at the Hebo Café, when needed, plowed the fields, and tended the crops.

Then came the really big news, with drawings of little hearts on the paper: Nick was coming home on leave! He had finished Basic Training and would be home for the Fourth of July weekend. And the last sentence of the note was the most encouraging of all. Chief Jacobs had promised Helen that he would arrange to have Ruth at home for that weekend, as well! How sweet was that?

After all that good news, Ruth mustered her courage and read Roy's letters. They were both short and disappointing. He made no mention of their stolen kisses or his promise to come for a visit. Instead, he wrote about the weather, the crops, and what the convict crew was doing at the County Farm. Even his closing was an insult: 'Best Regards.' "Best Regards this!" she yelled angrily, with her middle finger in the air. "What about us?"

Sadly, Ruth watched both of his letters burn up in her wood stove. What had happened to her Deputy Roy? She couldn't get him out of her head.

The last letter she read was from *Little Bird* at the Crow's Nest. Margaret was chatty and curious about how Ruth was doing at Hebo Butte. "The first few weeks are the worst. Get to know the animals that come by for a visit. They are fun to watch and worth studying."

*Little Bird* also suggested that, after the evening check-ins, Ruth should change to a radio frequency of 29 MHZ and she would do the same. That way, they could talk to each other without the other lookouts listening in. Ruth liked the idea. That night, for the first time, she talked with Margaret on the radio. As it turned out, the two women had much in common, and they soon became fast radio friends. It was nice to hear a female voice again, and they would talk into the night, hand-cranking the generator until their arms gave out.

With the Summer Solstice on June 21st, the weather turned from wet and cool to hot and dry. The summer fire season was upon the lookouts and, after two thunder storms, *Tonto* on Thunder Mountain reported a smoky fire and *Eagle Eye* on Buzzard Butte did the same. The two fires were quickly put out by ground crews and the blimps. The damage to the forests was only marginal, and the Air Station proved its worth by helping douse the flames. With the warm, dry weather, everyone was put on the alert, scrutinizing the forest day and night. There would be no more leaving the towers for long walks in the woods.

There was a pounding on Ruth's door.

"Wake-up, sunshine. It's time to go to work."

The door was locked on the inside, and the wooden shutters were closed on the outside, to keep the daylight out. The nest was all locked up tight.

"Ruthie, let me in. I need coffee, girl."

Winnie started barking.

Roy pounded on the door again. "Come on, Ruthie! We have things to do and places to go. Open the damn door, girl."

Prodded by Winnie's barks, Ruth stumbled out of bed and made her way to the door, where she unfastened the inside latch and opened it a crack. Then, seeing Roy, she shaded her eyes with one hand and opened the door farther with the other. "What are you doing here?" she demanded, yawning.

"I have a truck load of convicts downstairs," Roy said, opening the outside shutters. "We came up here to do a day's work, and I thought you might make us a pot of coffee."

Ruth retreated from the doorway and retrieved her pocket watch from the table, her head spinning. Wasn't she supposed to be mad at Roy? "It's not even 8 o'clock yet. I still have an hour before check-in."

"We start at 7 o'clock on the farm," Roy stated flatly, glancing at Ruth. "By the way, I like your night-clothes. You have a nice figure, Ruthie."

Aghast, she realized she was standing in front of

Roy in only her chemise and panties. Her face turned crimson and she dove for her sleeping bag and clothes. "Did you come up here just to get an eyeful?" Ruth demanded, stepping into her overalls.

"I hadn't realized how pretty you are, so sweet and young."

"Why are you here, Roy?" she asked again, lacing up her tennis shoes.

"Official orders from Chief Jacobs. By the way, there are six of us, seven if you want a cup of coffee, too. Is that okay?"

"How nice of you to include me. After all, it is my coffee," Ruth replied sarcastically.

"Good," Roy smiled. "I'll get the stove going and put the pot on while you finish dressing. Probably not a good idea for the convicts to see you in your underwear."

"How thoughtful of you," Ruth snapped back. "Now tell me why you're here."

While the coffee brewed, Roy explained why they had been sent. Chief Jacobs had learned from *Pops,* at Nestucca Dunes, that he had also found an abandoned copper pot still hidden in the bushes near his tower. With that discovery, along with some reports of poaching, the chief sent Roy and another Deputy, Sam Larson, with four members of the convict crew to investigate in and around all the Firewatch towers. They would look for any signs of intruders, and post warnings on the Federal lands. 'No Trespassing, Hunting or Fishing allowed without special permit issued by the order of the Chief Forester.'

"No telling what we might find. We'll spend the day searching up to the summit, then go to Nestucca Dunes next." Roy took the enamel pot off the stove. "Coffee's done. Let's take it down to the boys."

"I don't have seven tin cups," Ruth answered, wondering if she could possibly stay mad at Roy. He looked damned handsome in his summer uniform.

"Don't worry, we brought our own. The prisoners make mugs in their pottery class. It keeps them busy and out of trouble."

Ruth chuckled. "Pottery class! How about basket weaving? You must have a jailhouse full of real desperados."

Moving down the outside staircase, with Roy carrying the coffee pot, they found Deputy Larson and the four prisoners scattered around the property, smoking and talking to each other. Handing the full pot of coffee to Ruth, Roy blew his whistle and yelled out, "Gather around the truck with mugs in hand. This is the last coffee you'll see today."

As the men moved to the truck, Ruth noticed the prisoners wore black overalls, not their normal striped prison uniforms. That was when she also noticed the ugly face of one of the inmates. It was Mr. Maggot! She almost dropped the coffee pot in surprise, but recovered in time to take a firmer grip, determined not to give in to her fear.

As the men stood in line, mugs in hand, she walked down the ranks, pouring the coffee without saying a word. When she approached Maggot, he held his mug out and said, leering, "I glazed a mermaid on my mug, thinking of you." He brandished his cup, which did indeed bear a crude likeness of a mermaid with big tits. "She reminds me of you, Goldilocks."

Ruth forced herself to make eye contact with him and saw that he was even bigger and more brutal looking than she'd recalled. His arms were covered in tattoos, and his deep set blue eyes seemed as vacant as a desert sky. All in all, Mr. Maggot was the most threatening character she had ever seen. He made the Wicked Witch from the Oz movie look like an angel.

"How nice of you to think of me," Ruth said, her hand trembling as she poured the brew. "The coffee is hot and sassy, just like me, so be careful what you wish for."

Mr. Maggot took a sip, then another, and turned to Deputy Roy. "My little mermaid makes good coffee. I'll chop her more firewood before we leave."

Roy nodded at Ruth and whispered in her ear. "Yep, that's how to handle Mr. Maggot. Befriend your enemies and challenge your friends. It works almost every time."

Ruth poured herself a cup of coffee and looked Maggot squarely in the eye. "Thank you, sir. I can always use more wood."

As soon as the crew was done with their coffee, they split-up into two groups. Sam took his group searching up the log roads to the summit, while Roy took Ruth and his group down the trail to the lake.

A few hours later, walking back towards her tower, Ruth pointed out the tree stump where she'd had the run-in with the cougar. "Roy, your whistle saved my life that day. I will always be in your debt."

Roy shrugged his shoulders. "The power of the whistle is just an old hunting trick my father taught me, many years ago."

They moved up the trail, and Ruth confided, "I got

your two letters, Roy. I burned them in my wood stove."

"Why would you do that?" he asked, looking perplexed.

"If I wanted to know about the weather and the crops, I'd read my Almanac. You said nothing about us. Your letters were about as romantic as a dead fish."

Roy stopped and lifted one of his hands. "Wait a minute! Your father told me to stay away from you. And I promised him I would."

"Well, you promised *me* you'd come for a visit, but you never did. Do you have a new girlfriend?"

Roy turned to Ruth. "I'm not going to lie to you. My old girl friend from college moved back to town recently. I took her to lunch at the Hebo Café. She's a nice girl, more my age than you are. But she's just not right for me. She is looking for a Soldier Boy with a life insurance policy. That's surely not me."

Ruth cringed when she learned they had gone to the Hebo Café. Now Lucy Wilson and her mother, Alice, would know that Deputy Roy was available. It would be all over town by now, and here she was, stuck in the woods all summer. Ruth was jealous of Lucy, and that was a new feeling for her.

Disconcerted, she changed the subject. "I got some great news the other day. My brother Nick is coming home on leave. He'll be here for the Fourth of July weekend and I'll be with him. I hope you'll come by and meet him. He's one of three most important men in life."

"Who are the other two?"

"You and Oscar of course, but for different reasons. You are my mentor, helping me become a woman, and my

Father is teaching me how to live with disappointments."

"Those are tall orders Ruthie," Roy said as they came to the trailhead. "I don't know anything about the whims of women, but don't give up on me. I'll write you some fancy letters. And I'll visit you soon."

Sneaking behind a tree, Ruth kissed Roy on the lips again.

No one saw anything, that day – neither her kiss nor any sign of intruders. In fact, the only thing the crew accomplished that morning was a few dozen posters nailed to trees and a half cord of firewood stacked neatly underneath her tower, thanks to Mr. Maggot. And what had Ruth accomplished? Well, she had conquered her fear of Mr. Maggot, that morning, and she'd patched up her romance with Roy. Or had she?

Counting the days until the Fourth of July, Ruth kept a close eye on the tinder-dry forest. The state and county had both issued a moratorium on fireworks and closed the forest for the coming holiday to everyone except the loggers, firefighters, and lookouts. There were long, hot days and longer nights, with her tin roof turning her hut into an oven. She prayed for rain and the safe return of her brother.

# Chapter Eleven

## Fury

The Fourth of July fell on a Saturday in 1942. With the weather cool and the winds light, the cloudy morning gave way to a sunny afternoon. The seas that day were calm as well, and it seemed as if a lazy day was ahead for the Nelson family after several months of separation from their son Nick.

Private Nick Nelson, USMC, had made it home from Camp Pendleton on Friday afternoon, and his father Oscar picked him up at the bus stop in Tillamook. After eight weeks of boot camp, Nick looked so healthy and handsome in his Marine uniform that Oscar took him to a few taverns to show him off. While Nick wasn't legally old enough to drink beer, most of the bartenders looked the other way for any man in uniform.

When the Nelson men finally arrived at Shangri-La, both men were sauced and delighted to find Ruth setting the table for dinner. Nick and she hugged gleefully, chattering like a pair of magpies. He wanted to know all about the Fire Towers and her new job, while she wanted to know about boot camp and being a Marine.

As they devoured one of Helen's finest meals, a leg of lamb with mint jelly, Nick told them about his experiences at Camp Pendleton. His stories were graphic and full of barracks talk for which Helen scolded him, but she listened to every word.

"After special weapons training, I will know how to kill those f*** slant-eyed bastards. No mercy from me, just blood and guts. The only good Jap is a dead Jap. You wait and see."

Ruth was surprised by his hate-filled stories laced with foul language and lewd comments. Nick had changed: he was a solider now, looking to pick a fight. After Pearl Harbor, what had she expected? But the look in his eyes was a little scary, so she changed the subject.

"I have a new friend. I hope you can meet him tomorrow. His name is Roy Adams and he's a deputy sheriff, a real nice guy. He took me to my graduation dance."

"Was he a good dancer? Nick asked.

She smiled at her brother. "He's no jive bomber, but he's handsome and friendly."

Oscar shook his head with a frown. "I told you, Ruthie, stay away from that punk. He's just a horny toad, out for what he can get."

"He's a nice man," Helen said, clearing the table. "Let Nick make up his own mind about Deputy Roy."

Soon, the women were in the kitchen, doing the dishes, while Nick and Oscar sat at the table and argued about the war. It was just like old times, with the men drinking and talking while the girls did the work.

When they were done, mother and daughter walked

outside to watch the sunset. As they stood by the barn in the remains of a beautiful day, Helen removed a small black cigar from her apron and lit it with a wooden match. "Have you been kissing Roy?"

Ruth blushed in the sunlight. "He kissed me once, and I kissed him back. Nothing else, mom."

"Good," Helen answered, blowing smoke into the still air. "I want to tell you about men and your virginity."

"We had this talk before, mother. I know my way around the barnyard."

"Not when it comes to men. Kiss them and hold them. That's okay. But don't let them hump you. Save your virginity for your husband. That's how you protect yourself from becoming pregnant."

Her mother talked about sex in a cold, stark tone, as if she was talking about a recipe. Where were her emotions, her passions? Ruth didn't quite understand her. She seemed to lack any liking for romance.

Nestucca Bay, where both Nestucca Rivers empty into the ocean, was where they spent the next afternoon. It was also the location of the Nestucca Dunes tower and the nest of Henry Hoyt. Ruth had seen his tower from her blimp ride but soon she would be standing on the beach, looking up at it.

That next morning, while Helen and Ruth cooked, and packed a picnic basket, Oscar and Nick drove to Hebo for a case of beer and a bag full of contraband fireworks. The last thing Nick purchased was an American flag on a pole, which he planned to plant in the sands of the beach when he lit his fireworks at dusk. He was so proud of being a Marine that he also planned to spend the day in his uniform.

The Nelson family, along with their friends, the Wilsons from the Hebo Café, arrived at the bay in the afternoon to build windbreaks out of log snags, start bonfires, and set up camp on the sandy shore. The weather was clear and warm. Children laughed and played, while neighbors talked of their crops and of the war as the sun slowly crept across the sky. With all the disappointing war news, everyone at the beach seemed determined to make this day a real Fourth of July special. It was a day for celebration, with or without fireworks.

With the camp all set up, Oscar took Nick to walk the sand spits, talking with old neighbors and new friends, showing off Nick in his uniform. Everyone seemed impressed with another local boy going off to war. The beer flowed and the wine lubricated. It was a proud occasion for both Oscar and Nick.

While this was happening, Ruth walked her mother over to Henry Hoyt's Fire Tower, explaining to her how she lived in a similar tower at Hebo Butte. "It's much the same as my nest, only his is ten feet taller."

That's when Henry appeared on his catwalk, smoking his pipe. He invited them up to his hut for a better view, and the ladies were delighted to accept his invitation.

To be fifty feet up in a tower can really change ones perspective of the surroundings. So it was with *Pop*'s nest. He had an almost unlimited view of the ocean, much like a lighthouse. And his inland views of the forest lands, from south to north, were outstanding. He even pointed out to Ruth his view of her tower on Hebo Butte. "On clear days,

I can see you out on your catwalk, working."

Ruth flinched at his comment, reminding herself always to cover up when she was on the catwalk, since she'd never know who might be watching.

Henry was a gracious host, serving them coffee and cookies, then showing Helen how use the Fire Finder. They talked at great length about living in their towers and how they communicated with the outside world. "It's a lonely life out here, but spiritual, as well, living so close to God's handiwork."

When the time came to leave, Helen thanked Henry for his hospitality and invited him to their picnic table. "Come by anytime, *Pops*. We have fried chicken, Norwegian potato salad, lutefisk, pickled salmon, and cold beers. You won't go home hungry from my picnic basket."

It was late in the afternoon by the time Ruth and her mother returned to their camp, where they found Nick and Deputy Roy sitting on a log snag, drinking beer and talking. Roy was wearing his summer uniform, and Ruth was pleased to see her dreamboat again.

Grinning, he stood up as they approached. "I found Oscar and Nick out on the beach, talking with folks, and they pointed me to your camp. Nick was kind enough to show me the way."

"Is my husband still sober?" Helen asked Roy with a frown.

"About halfway, ma'am," he answered. "Maybe you should put some coffee on."

"Why are you in uniform?" Ruth asked, with a puzzled face.

"Got duty all weekend. But I wanted to come by and meet Nick."

"We've got a lot in common," Nick said, still resting on the snag. "We both graduated from Tillamook High School, just two years apart."

That was when Oscar staggered into camp, red-faced and drunk. "What would you have in common with a shit-head like Roy?" he asked his son, then turned to shout at the deputy. "I told you to stay away from Ruth, yet here you are. What part of 'stay away' don't you understand?"

Helen was on her knees next to the fire, putting the coffee pot on to the heat. She looked up at her husband, shaking her head. "He came to meet Nick, not to argue with you. Leave the deputy alone."

"Come on, Dad," Nick joined in. "It's the Fourth of July. Let bygones be bygones. We are all Americans here today, wanting to defeat the Japs."

Oscar threw his empty beer bottle at Helen. It missed her but it shattered on the rocks. "Stay out of this, woman," he shouted, his words slurring. "She's my daughter." He moved closer to Roy, his fist clenched as if he were about to take a swing at him.

The Wilsons had the campfire next to them and were watching the altercation. Fuming, Oscar pounded his fist into his open hand. "Get the f*** out of here before I spread you out on the fire."

Roy glared at him. "I don't fight cripples. It wouldn't be fair." Then he held up a placating hand. "The last time we talked, I promised you I wouldn't see your daughter socially again, and I haven't. My visit today is official business. I have a sealed envelope for Ruth from

Chief Jacobs. He asked me to deliver it, and I have, so I will be moving on now."

Calm and reason saved the day, with Roy talking Oscar out of his anger without throwing a single punch. He was one sweet talker.

With that thought in mind, Ruth walked with him to his Studebaker, apologizing again for her father. "You don't have to leave. We could walk up the beach and get away from Oscar," Ruth pleaded.

"I don't think so," Roy answered, getting into his truck. "If I don't leave now, I'll spend the evening writing out citations for illegal fireworks, which I don't want to do. You just enjoy the show and being with your brother."

"We never seem to have any time for us," Ruth answered sadly.

"I have a day off, next Friday, and I'll come up to Hebo Butte for a visit. I promise.

With the sun setting, Nick pushed his flagpole into the sand next to their campsite and lit his punk from the fire. Ruth stood next to him, examining the fireworks in the sack, while Helen cleaned up from the picnic. Her meal had been outstanding but the mood of her diners had been dampened by Oscar's angry words. Ruth and Nick had been humiliated again by their father! Now they were determined to let their fireworks do the talking, with roman candles, skyrockets, and pinwheels. It was a sky show of explosions, colors and clamor not unlike the many battles Nick would soon face as he island-hopped across the Pacific.

As for the sealed envelope Roy had brought to Ruth, it was from the county and contained her pay in cash with a reminder he would pick her up on Tuesday morning for her return to Hebo Butte. Nick was leaving on the same morning for his return trip to Camp Pendleton. That gave the brother and sister only two more days of catching up before reality would set in again.

**Contraband Fireworks over Nestucca Bay July 1942**

# Chapter Twelve

## Fast Track

The only welcoming face back at her tower was Winnie's. Chief Jacobs had watched over the dog and her nest during Ruth's four day leave. While he was on the station, he had reported smoke and flames in the Pleasant Valley area, and that was confirmed by *Eagle Eye* at Buzzard Butte and *Little Bird* at Crow's Nest. Within the hour, two fire trucks were on the scene, and the fire was under control in less than two hours. Three different bearings from three different Fire Finders: that was triangulation, just how the tower system was supposed to work! Ruth was only disappointed she hadn't been there to make the initial call.

Now that the fires had been secured, Ruth hunkered down with catwalks roughly every two hours and more frequent bike rides in the mornings and evenings. She was determined to do her part with the next reported fire.

Like the ticking of her pocket watch, time flew by from one routine to the next, while the weather remained hot and the rains long gone. With the boiling, sticky days, she found herself hiking to the lake for more water two or three times a day. She even put together the wood and rubber bathtub she had stowed in the storeroom. The next day, she made three more trips to the lake, and took a bath under the stars that night. Using the bath salts her mother had given her, she felt decadent for enjoying such a luxury when the other lookouts were sweating it out. When she finished with her bath, she smelled so good that even the birds started chirping again.

True to his word, Roy pulled up to her tower that next Friday afternoon. When he got out of his truck, he noticed the rubber bathtub with the soapy water still inside. He smiled, looking up at the tower and honked his horn. Ruth appeared and smiled back down at him. "You're here just like you promised. Come on up."

"Crank down the big wire basket first. Then come down and join me. I come bearing gifts."

"Oh, I like the sound of that," she answered, cranking down the big basket. "It's hot as hell in the nest."

As Ruth made her way down the stairs with Winnie in her arms, Roy loaded two fat duffel bags into the wire basket and secured the load with ropes.

"What's in the bags?" Ruth asked, approaching his truck. She was all decked out in khaki shorts, a black halter-top, and leather sandals, with her yellow hair up in a bun. Even in the sweltering heat, she looked as fresh as the morning dew.

"The bags are for later. Look what's in the back of my truck."

She moved to the pickup and looked in the back.

It was empty, except for two fishing poles and a tackle box. He joined her, with a serious expression. Roy came to attention and gave her a hand salute. "I'm here on official business for the county. The boys at Fish and Wildlife need to know how the fishing is, on Lake Hebo, so

I've been dispatched to ascertain that information." He finished his salute with a wink of his eye. "So we are going fishing and I'm making you a candlelight dinner. Are you game for such an adventure, m'lady?"

Ruth nodded her approval with a big smile. "As long as we are back in two hours for my next catwalk."

Roy grabbed the poles and the tackle box, and they were off down the trail as he chuckled and said, "Just remember, this isn't a social call, ma'am. Just doing my duty for the county."

That short trip to the lake was the first time Ruth had been fishing since moving into her tower. She had seen the fish jumping in the water many times before. Now she would see if she could catch any.

With the ducks and eagles watching, they used the dingy as Roy baited their hooks and gave her instructions on casting. It didn't take long. With the bite on, they pulled in three fat trout within half hour.

Roy cleaned the fish on the lakeshore, using the knife he had given Ruth. After they finished, they took a dip in the lake to cool off. Giggling and splashing water on each other, he kissed her once and she kissed him back.

Later in the afternoon, with the fish in the tackle box and filled water bags in their hands, they hiked the trail back to her tower. She had procrastinated such a fishing trip for weeks and, thanks to Roy, she had the fish to prove her skills.

As Ruth roamed her catwalk, Roy cranked up the bags and dragged them into nest. While he opened the duffels, he shouted out the contents. "Two more webbed folding chairs, for starters. The one you have now is as hard as a rock."

"Good!" she shouted back from outside. "Did you bring me a bigger cooking table?"

"I did, and a bag of tin plates, cups, and flatware. Oh, and a new coffee pot. Your old pot makes lousy coffee. I don't care what Mr. Maggot says."

Ruth came back into the nest with her binoculars around her neck. "It's cooling off, out there. Why are you giving me all these gifts?"

"That's just one bag, and you have a birthday coming up. The second bag has all the ingredients I need for my candle-light dinner."

Ruth regarded him with fondness in her eyes. "I like it when we spend time together."

"So do I," Roy answered. Then, looking flustered, he said, "Well, I better get the dinner going."

With only one candle burning on the table, and one turned-down lantern burning over the stove, Roy cooked a fish fry fit for a king: filleted trout sautéed with fresh butter and herbs, garnished with glazed red potatoes and pastries he had purchase that morning. The last item he put on the table was a bottle of red Victory Wine, which he opened and served with the dinner.

It was truly a gourmet meal in the middle of the wilderness. Ruth was impressed! Her mother would be proud of Roy, even with the bottle of wine. As they talked in the candle light, Ruth couldn't keep her eyes off of him. He was honest and handsome, with a warm personality. He was a man true to his word, and she felt comfortable asking him anything.

"I have a question, Roy. When we kiss, your tongue tries to part my lips. Why is that?"

Roy took a sip of wine from his tin cup. "I guess it's because I kiss French-style."

"French-style? What's that? I only know Norwegian style."

Roy smiled at her, "French style is open-mouth kissing. I've heard that the French have been doing it that way for hundreds of years."

Ruth took a drink from her tin cup and scooted her chair next him.

"Okay, give me a French kiss and I'll see if I like it."

He put both of his hands on her face and pulled her closer to him, whispering, "You look so beautiful in candle light." Then he kissed her French style for the longest moment. When they parted, she had a flushed face, and took another drink from her cup. "I think I understand now. Those Frenchmen are very clever." She cleared her throat. "Are you a virgin?"

Roy thought for a moment, then shook his head. "A gentleman doesn't discuss such things. And ladies shouldn't ask such questions."

"I'm just curious about you and other girls. You seem to know so much."

"Well, there were other girls in college. Mostly, we just kissed and hugged. Nothing serious."

"So you did nothing?"

"No Some girls petted, and others spooned. It was a way to get to know one another."

"You mean petting like a dog? And what's

spooning?"

"Spooning is like a cuddle and a hug and maybe a little bit more," Roy answered. "But "Ruthie these are questions you should be asking your mother, not me."

Ruth stood blowing out the candle. "No! I want you to teach me how to pet and spoon. If other girls are doing it, I should know how to, as well." She put her hand out to Roy. "Let me introduce you to my sleeping bag. We won't go all the way. I just need to know."

"Ruth Ann, this is a bad idea!" Roy answered. "Your father would kill me."

"He's not here," She answered with an alluring face.

They slept all night together, talking, exploring, and kissing each other. It was sensual but not sexual: a safe and satisfying experience with no fear or worry.

The next morning, they had breakfast together. It was Roy's day off, and they planned to drive around the mountain, looking for other ponds where they might like to fish. The sun was up and the day looked to be hot again.

At 9 o'clock, Ruth checked in with her morning report. All seemed normal from the lookouts, with only a few aircraft and two ships tallied. The last report was from *Eagle Eye* at Buzzard Butte. He told the network that he had found a large, metallic balloon hung up in a tree next to his tower. He said he was going to climb the tree to retrieve it. The radio operator at the Fire Station told everyone to stand by.

Moments later, Chief Jacobs was on radio. He advised everyone to stand down from talking about or touching any balloons found in trees. "These might be Japanese weather balloons, so don't touch them until we check them out." His final remark was quite guarded: "If anyone has contact with Deputy Roy Adams, have him report immediately to the Sheriff's Office. This is not a drill. Fire Station over and out."

Roy and Ruth were bewildered by the urgency of the message. No one knew he was at Hebo Butte, and they had promised each other that no one ever would. After one last kiss, Roy climbed into his truck and drove away. Something was wrong. But what?

The answer to that question came early the next morning, when Roy returned with *Tonto*, *Pops,* and Doctor Wong in his truck. Moments after their arrival, Chief Jacobs drove in with *Little Bird, Eagle Eye,* and Commander Cash. The commander called everyone together, standing around Chief Jacobs's truck. "Sorry for the early morning wake-up call. I have news we cannot talk about on the radio or with anyone outside this group. What I have to say is a Military Secret and cannot be divulged to anyone else, ever! The Imperial Japanese Navy has developed a secret weapon capable of burning down all the forests of the Pacific Northwest."

That statement captured the immediate attention of all the lookouts, and their faces took on expressions of deep concern.

The commander reached into the bed of the truck and lifted out a partially deflated paper balloon with wires below the gasbag attached to a metal canister. The entire weapon was about ten foot tall.

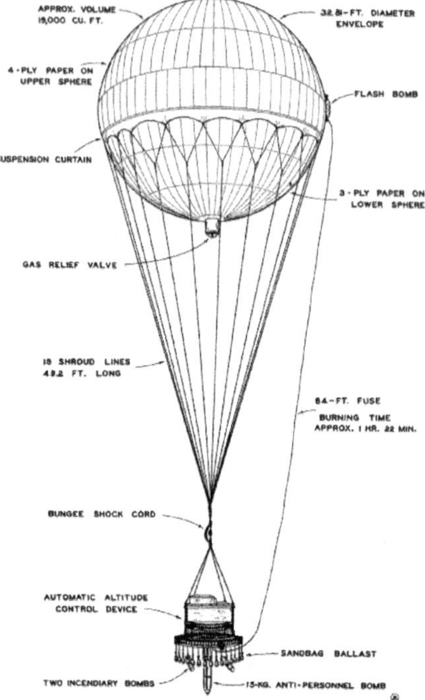


**FU-GO Bomb**

"The canister at the bottom of this balloon is an incendiary bomb, booby-trapped to go off upon landing. Our military thinks there may be thousands of these little *Devil Bombs* on their way to our forests. The Japanese call these bombs FU-GO they come in all different sizes. If you see them in the sky, report them. If you see them in a tree or floating in river or a lake, report them. Don't play cowboy and try to shoot them down or disturb them in any way. For radio purposes only, we will call these new weapons 'pineapples.' Are there any questions?

"Tokyo Rose said the other night that the Doolittle Raid only burnt down civilian housing, and that Japan was coming after our homes now," Ruth said, looking over the balloon. "Do you think she was talking about these *FU-GO Bombs*?"

"You listen to Tokyo Rose?" Roy asked.

"Yes I do," Ruth answered. "Someone once told me to befriend my enemies and challenge my friends."

"We don't know what that bitch was talking about." Commander Cash said. "But we do know of a few fatalities and some fires caused by these balloon bombs down state."

"I didn't read about these bombs in the newspaper," *Pops* said.

"And you won't," Cash answered. "The Government censors put a lid on all the news stories. The last thing we need to do is give credibility to Tokyo Rose, or frighten the locals. That's why this is all top secret."

*Eagle Eye* reached out and touched the balloon. "Is this the gasbag that was up in the tree, next to my tower?

"Yes," Commander Cash answered. "We got it down from there early this morning, while you were sleeping. One of my ordinance officers disarmed it. Turns out it had a faulty booby-trap. We were lucky."

"Wait a minute," *Little Bird* said, with a curious face. "It's over five thousand miles from here to Japan. How can such a tiny little balloon fly that far?"

Doctor Wong answered her question. "We find Japanese glass-floats on our beaches all the time. They float all the way here on the prevailing currents. These pineapples do the same with high altitude winds known as the Trade Winds. Some of these balloons might be able to fly as far as the East Coast. No one knows for sure."

The Firewatchers and Navy bosses talked about the balloon bombs for over an hour, mapping out strategies and procedures for dealing with the pineapples. It was frightening to think that one of those balloons could land on a house and burn it down without a warning. These silent pineapples had to be stopped, but how?

During the tailgate meeting, Ruth had to restrain herself from staring at Roy. The last thing she needed was for some knucklehead to think she and he were an item. But as the meeting broke up, Roy walked over to her and slipped a note into her hand with a wink. “Here’s the radio frequency for Voice of America. Don’t waste your time listening to Tokyo Rose.”

Ruth took the paper and put it in her pocket. “Thank you, deputy. Do you have time for coffee?”

“No,” he answered. “We have to get everybody back to their nests.”

Moments later when everyone was gone, Ruth read the slip of paper from her pocket: I will count the days until our next candlelight dinner. The sight and scent of you I will never forget. Stay safe and wear your whistle, Love Roy.

Wow, he said he said ‘love’! Life was swell!

# Chapter Thirteen

## Big Blow

Every good seafarer knows that the Columbia River Bar is one of the most treacherous Bar crossings in the world. That's why there were three lighthouses and a lightship standing guard at the entrance to the river. The Columbia Bar is the doorway to the graveyard of the Pacific. Nearly constant storms blow up from the south, with immense tides and deep undertows. Add to that the sheer volume of water from the Columbia River, and the Bar becomes choked with tall waves and violent shoals. The Pacific Northwest is notorious for her storms.

On the evening of the tailgate meeting, the lookouts checked-in on the radio, with no mention of pineapples or any threatening fires. All seemed peaceful until the Air Station operator issued a brief weather alert: 'The Coos Bay Weather Station is reporting a high wind warning from the south-southwest at 40 mph with gusts to 65 mph. This blow is heading north. It is advised that all ships batten down the hatches and seek safe harbor.' That was the extent of the warning. Ruth took special note of the winds, which could be carrying more *Devil Bombs*.

With twilight fast approaching, Ruth and Winnie went downstairs for one last walk around the compound. As she waited for his return, she dumped out the bathtub water and carried the empty tub into the storeroom. She moved her bicycle into storage, as well. Looking around the grounds, she spotted nothing else that might fly away.

After securing the door to the storeroom with the iron latch, she and her dog returned upstairs. There was a cool breeze swirling around her catwalk so she closed all the windows and shutters, then locked all the doors. With the new black-out order for the coast, the darkness outside was like a coal pit. Using her only flashlight, Ruth crawled into her sleeping bag and said to her dog, "There's nothing to worry about. We'll just let this storm blow by."

With Winnie curled up next to her, she was ready for dreamland and whatever else Mother Nature might have in mind. On this windy evening, her thoughts focused on Roy and the night before, not the tempest brewing outside.

As she closed her eyes to the symphony of the storm, it started to blow, low and slow, with a few pebbles pelting the walls of her hut while swirling winds whistled around the posts that held up her platform. Then trees began to sway, with broken branches, flying limbs, and the sound of rocks and stones dancing on her metal roof. After that came the shaking of her tower, the sound of breaking glass, and the intensifying roar of the winds.

At 3AM, Ruth woke to a gust like an earthquake shaking the tower, with winds swirling around her catwalk. She was frightened and Winnie was trembling. With the storm continuing to build, it was still pitch-black outside. Ruth tried to go back to sleep but to no avail. With her mind racing as her hut swayed, she said to her dog, "We worried about fires, when the real villain here is the wind. But this will soon blow by."

Then a tree next to her tower came crashing down, with a loud thud and a cracking of timbers that shook her room. That was it! At first light, they would have to get out of the tower before it collapsed like an accordion. This was no time to dilly dally.

There was color in the eastern sky about 5AM, but the howling winds and blowing debris made it difficult to see the horizon. Using her flashlight, Ruth got dressed and packed a small emergency kit of water and food. Her plan was to walk down the mountain and then on to Shangri-La. That would be a safe place. But at first light, when she held Winnie in her arms and exited the hut, she was pelted with wind-flung debris that stung like bees. She covered the dog with her jacket and ran down the stairs, dodging and weaving the airborne sticks and stones. Once on the ground, she ran for the storage room to get out of the wind.

When she reached it, she was dismayed to find the door open, banging against the walls as it was buffeted by the wind. Ruth rushed inside and closed the door as best she could, now that its iron latch was bent.

That was when she heard a strange sound. Turning from the door, she aimed her flashlight and spotted a little bear cub, about the size of Winnie, devouring potatoes from a burlap sack. Only a few months old, it was a cute little critter but as dangerous as the storm. Where was its mother? Still holding her yapping dog in her arms, Ruth swung the flashlight beam to see whether the mother sow was in the storage room.

It wasn't! Opening the door to the outhouse, Ruth set Winnie inside the little room. "You stay here. I'll be right back," she said, and closed the outhouse door.

Soon the sow was at the storage door pounding on the timbers and roaring loudly over the sounds of the storm. The sow wanted in, for her cub and for the potatoes. The iron door latch was bent and wouldn't withstand a long onslaught, pitted against the determined weight of the mother bear.

*Give her what she wants!* The words ran through Ruth's head. She looked at the little cub, busily eating the spuds. *How do you pick it up?* She pondered that as she put the whistle between her lips, and the answer came to her. *By the scruff of the neck!*

Grabbing the cub, she carried it to the door and peered through a crack in the timbers, waiting for the sow to approach the door again. As she did, Ruth unlatched the door and threw it open, blowing her whistle as loudly as she could. The stark, high-pitched sounds startled the sow, who hesitated and turned as if to run. As she did, Ruth stepped outside, and placed the cub on the ground. Then, closing the door quickly, she rushed back into the storeroom and filled her hands with potatoes. Returning to the door, she opened it and threw the spuds at the sow and her cub. Finally, heart racing, she latched the door again from the inside and crossed to the commode to join Winnie inside the little room. "I told you I'd be right back. Roy's little whistle saved our bacon again," she said to her dog. Her words sounded confident, but Ruth was exhausted, mentally and physically, still trembling as the winds howled outside.

The end of the storm came a few hours later, bringing clear skies and silent breezes. Exiting the storeroom, Ruth found that the bear and her cub were long gone, along with her potatoes. But the tower was still standing, and the roof remained on. Overhead, it was as if nothing had happened, but the grounds around the tower were covered in uprooted trees, broken branches, and piles of debris.

Ruth picked her way through it all to the foot of the stairs and began to climb. The views from ground level had been chaotic enough, as if a tornado had touched down. But once she returned to the nest and looked around, the views from the catwalk looked as if someone had played pick-up sticks with the trees. Many were strewn on the ground, at all different angles. The forest looked like so much kindling, waiting to be lit.

Wiping tears from her eyes, Ruth went inside, turned on her radio, and dialed in *Little Bird* at the Crow's Nest. No answer.

Next, she tried the Fire Station. No answer.

Finally she connected with the Air Station. The power and telephones lines were out for the entire county, but the Navy was up and running, using a generator. The Fire Station wasn't operating because they had run out of gasoline during the storm. The main roads were closed because of fallen trees, and some of the bridges had collapsed.

It was a mess, up and down the coast. The winds had blown at over 85 miles an hour and, unlike most gales, there had been no rain after the storm. The forests were still tinder dry, with the highest warnings of wild fires.

The radio operator told Ruth that she was isolated and should stay in place. “It will be a few days before we can get a crew up to rescue you. Over and out” he said in a condescending voice.

“Sailor, I don’t need rescuing, not by you or anyone else. Just tell the Fire Station that I checked in. Over and out!”

The storm had done some damage to her nest. The wind howling through her chimney had spread a layer of stove soot over the entire room. Additionally, two windows had broken panes, and three of the wooden shutters needed repair. But nothing else of a serious nature had happened, so Ruth rolled up her sleeves, opened all the windows and shutters, and went to work cleaning, fixing, and watching the landscape for any sign of smoke. Her plan was to stay in place. She worried about her family and Roy, but there wasn’t anything she could do currently to help them, or even to check on their wellbeing. She’d just have to stay busy.

By 9 o’clock that evening, the radio network was up and running again. To Ruth’s relief, each of the lookouts had survived the storm, and they told their stories of narrow escapes. Ruth told them about the mother bear and her cub, then poked fun at herself. “I threw potatoes at them and they scampered away. Better to be without my spuds than my dog.” They all laughed or chuckled, in need of some levity after the harrowing storm.

The last to speak from the Fire House was Roy. He told the lookouts that he had been out searching for a missing prisoner. Mr. Maggot had escaped from the County Farm during the gale. He was on the loose and might be coming the way of the towers to hide out.

Just the mention of his name set a chill down Ruth's spine. She wasn't afraid of him anymore, but she didn't want to deal with him.

"*Cloud Girl* here," she said into the microphone. "Any news about my family, deputy? Over."

"I'll check on them tomorrow. The roads up the mountain to Hebo Butte are impossible at this time, so stay put. Over and out."

Just hearing Roy's voice again assured Ruth that he was safe and doing his job. Hallelujah for that. But now it was time to get back to normal, watching the forest.

After the morning check-in, Ruth worked on more cleanup and repairs. She fixed the store-room door latch, then made wooden inserts to replace the broken windowpanes. She even walked to the lake, cleaning up the trail from the big blow down. When she arrived at the shoreline, she noticed that the birds had returned from wherever they had gone during the storm, and the forest was full of song again. The damage around the lake was only marginal, and the waters still looked enchanting.

**Blow Down From the Storm**

# Chapter Fourteen

**Fire & Fury**

A few days later, during one of her routine catwalks, Ruth noticed two blimps from the Air Station lifting off and heading north. There was something comforting about seeing those huge dirigibles in the sky. The county had suffered a devastating one-two punch from the big blow and now with the dry heat, there was no rain in the forecast.

With these thoughts in her head, she heard a call on the radio. She moved inside her nest to hear what was going on. It was the voice of *Pops,* at Nestucca Dunes. "Enemy plane contact – three Japanese PETE Type O aircraft flying north, fifteen miles south-southwest west of my location. Over."

He repeated his message, and Ruth replied by asking, "What is a PETE Type O? Over."

"Check your silhouettes. PETEs are Nip biplanes used for reconnaissance. Over." *Pops* answered.

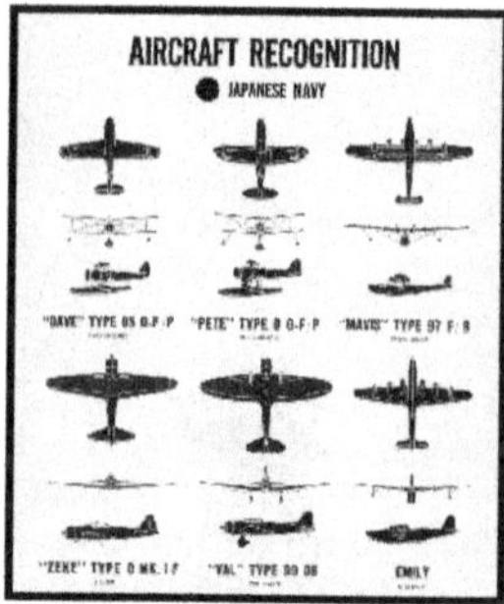


**Silhouette Book**

When Ruth found the right silhouette in her book, she couldn't believe her eyes. How could this be? She had only reported a handful of air contacts over the past six weeks, and now there were three enemy planes just off the coast!

Next, she heard Commander Cash's voice, trying to confirm *Pops'* report. "7th Fleet Command at the Presidio is reporting no enemy warships within a thousand miles of the Oregon coast. Are you sure these are floatplanes with Japanese markings? Over."

"Yes, sir!" Henry Hoyt answered firmly. "I about peed in my pants when I first saw them. Over."

Then *Tonto* clicked in. "Silver Cloud here. I can confirm *Pops'* report. The slant-eyes are five miles south of my position, three Jap seaplanes approaching the coast. Over."

Commander Cash signed off with instructions for the lookouts to keep feeding the coordinates of the aircraft to the Air Station.

With her book of aircraft silhouettes and binoculars in hand, Ruth returned to the catwalk to scan the forests and the skies. Aside from the many storm damaged timbers and a few pockets of wispy fog, everything looked normal to her. Then, with her binoculars pointing at *Pops'* tower, she saw two aircraft matching the seaplane description, flying north up the coast. But where was the third plane?

Moments later, the radio came back on. It was *Tonto*. "Thunder Mountain under attack from one PETE Type floatplane with Jap markings. They are dropping incendiary bombs on my forest and machine gunning my tower. I'm ducking for cover now. Over and out."

At the mention of incendiary bombs, Ruth tasted fear again. The tinder-dry forest could easily blow up in flames like so much kindling. She scanned north again and saw the lead blimp turn east for the coastal mountains. The second blimp did the same, gaining altitude. With the seaplanes hugging the coastline, they soon turned east at Cape Lookout, then headed for Pleasant Valley.

Ruth radioed their position. "Two aircraft just north of *Little Bird* at the Crow's Nest. They are coming your way, Margaret. Over."

"I see them," she answered, excitement in her voice. "The rear pilot is dropping silver canisters that are exploding on contact with the forest. Over."

"Look above you," Ruth said, holding the microphone button in. "Both blimps are coming after the planes. Take cover and stay low! Over."

Returning to her catwalk, Ruth saw flashes of fire coming from the forward machine gun positions of both blimps. As the blimps drove toward the two Nip seaplanes, she heard the *rat-a-tat-tat* of the machine guns. It was like a bird's eye view of David and Goliath battling it out over a sea of damaged trees. The two adversaries were still a few miles apart but getting closer with each tick of the clock. The lead PETE flew right over Margaret's nest, shooting as it passed by. Ruth could see the rear pilot dropping the canisters. It looked as if the plane was flying directly for Ruth next. She ran into her hut, found the pistol she had brought along, and ran out again, ready to use it.

Moments later, the lead floatplane flew directly over her tower without firing a shot or dropping any more canisters. Ruth pulled the trigger of her pistol three times but the flyby happened fast and she was sure she had missed the plane with all of her shots. Next, she looked up to see the last PETE flying over Margaret's tower, coming her way, but it had black smoke and flames streaming from its cowling. One of the blimps must have shot it up! As the plane struggled for altitude, the rear pilot dropped one last canister then bailed out. She watched his white silk parachute float to the forest floor.

Cocking her pistol again, Ruth waited for the second plane to fly by or crash. With a roaring, sputtering engine, emitting smoke and flames, the plane made it over the top of her tower, heading south. It flew by so close that Ruth could almost reach out and touch the pilot in his open cockpit. She fired three bullets at the airplane, but again it happened with blinding speed.

**Mitsubishi "PETE" was a Japanese reconnaissance Floatplane used during World War II**

She waited and listened, a few moments after the flyover, she heard a loud crash. What now? The plane wreck could start another fire.

She rushed back inside and keyed up the Air Station, "*Cloud Girl* here. Two flyovers at Hebo Butte. First PETE flying south with no visible damage. Second PETE with engine on fire crashed in the forest near Hebo Lake: Awaiting instructions. Over."

Chief Jacobs answered her call. "Fire units responding to Thunder Mountain and Crow's Nest. Are you safe, *Cloud Girl*? Over."

"On the beam. No damage to my tower, no threatening fires. Over." Ruth answered, with butterflies still in her stomach.

"Good," Chief Jacobs said. "Stay put and report what you see. Over."

"Are those pilots dead or alive? Over." someone asked from the Air Station.

"I don't know for sure," Ruth said, checking her

watch. "I saw one pilot parachute into the forest. As for the other one, I'll go see. We still have five hours of daylight. Over."

"No," Chief Jacobs said emphatically. "It's too dangerous. You stay in place. Over."

"I'll have to overrule you Jacobs," the voice of Commander Cash said. "We need all the intelligence we can gather about those planes and the pilots. Where the hell did these Japs come from, and how did they get here? Maybe we could drop in a volunteer with a rope ladder from one of our blimps. It's been done before. But it would have to be a volunteer. Over."

"I'll volunteer," Ruth heard herself say. "I'm already here and I'll report back with what I find. Over and out."

Chief Jacobs protested but Cash outranked everyone on site, Ruth was told what to look for in the wreckage: aircraft papers, maps, anything about the plane or the pilots. And she was given a time limit within which to report back. If they didn't hear from her in five hours, a blimp would be dispatched with another volunteer.

"You're our eyes and ears," Cash told her. "Don't let me down. Over and out."

Providing food and water, Ruth put Winnie in the storeroom and closed the door. He wasn't a happy dog but she was going to travel fast. Putting new batteries in her flashlight, she took an empty water bag, as well. She had traveled to the lake many times before and knew every shortcut and turn of the trail. The distance to the lake would take her just under a half hour, at a brisk walk. As she moved along the trail, her thoughts focused on the forest and what might happen because of the stealth attacks. The Japanese were a sneaky people. Nick called them Zipper Heads and Slant Eyes. Ruth just called them Japs.

When she got to the lakeshore, she could see the crashed floatplane at the far end of the lake. Its tail section was pointed high in the air, with its nose buried in the water at a 45-degree angle. The double wings on the left side of the plane had sheared off completely, while the right-side wings were crumpled like so much tin foil.

Ruth uncovered the dinghy and shoved it out onto the water. Then she got in and paddled toward the flightless bird. South of the lake, the sky had an orange glow from what she suspected was the Thunder Mountain fire. The lake itself was as quiet as a morgue. There were no birds chirping in the trees or swimming on the water. Everything seemed frozen in place. Even the breeze had died down to a dead calm. As she approached the mangled aircraft she had a spooky feeling. She had never seen a dead body before, and now she was about to be confronted with a dead Jap. Just that thought was creepy!

Paddling toward the damaged right wing, she saw that the forward cockpit was still open, with an object slumped over, inside the plane. She tied off her boat to one of the bent struts and lifted herself onto the stub of the wing next to the fuselage. Carefully, she moved to the empty rear cockpit and looked down inside the fuselage. Using her flashlight, she searched the dark chamber where the second pilot had jumped out.

Spotting a small pouch next to his seat, Ruth reached inside the cockpit and grabbed it. Inside the leather pouch, she found a few maps and some Japanese written documents that she couldn't read. She tossed the folder and its contents into her boat, then moved up to the open forward cockpit. Gathering her courage, she reached in and pulled the dead pilot upright in his seat.

The right side of his face was covered with blood, and there was a big welt above his ear. She looked at him, surprised that he looked so innocent and young. The left side of his face was un-bloodied, and his eyes were closed. His skin was tight and yellowish. Under his flight cap, his black hair was cut short. He was small, no bigger than she was, and he wore a brown flight suit, with a holstered pistol hanging off his shoulder. She quickly removed the gun and put it in her pocket.

Aided by the flashlight, Ruth searched the cockpit and found another pouch, next to the pilot's legs. It was bigger and fatter than the other one she'd found, and she reached inside to retrieve it. Just as she began to pull it up, the pilot's eyes flashed open, and he grabbed her wrist.

Ruth let out scream and nearly fell off the wing. She glared at him in fear and saw his eyes slide closed again, but his grip remained tight. Ruth had to pry his fingers off of her wrist, her heart racing. Why had she assumed he was dead?

With the fat pouch in hand, she dropped it into her boat, then gingerly checked his wrist for a pulse. She found only a slight response, and his breathing was shallow and unsteady. He could die at any moment. Now what?

She recalled what her brother Nick had said: *The only good Jap is a dead Jap.*

Ruth had little doubt that Nick would let him die in his plane. But this man could prove to be their best source of intelligence, if he lived. But how could she get him back to her tower for the Navy? The answer to that was obvious: drag him, carry him, or pull him. Ruth was a willful woman, and she knew what she had to do.

Reaching inside the cockpit, she unbuckled his seatbelt and lifted him partially out of his seat, then pulled him out of the bulkhead, dragging him down the wing to the waiting dinghy. Returning to the cockpit, she checked for anything else she might have overlooked, and found two items: a picture of two Japanese women: one dressed in a kimono, gum-stuck to the plane's dashboard, and a Christian cross dangling from a gold chain. She slipped both items into her pocket.

Paddling back across the lake, Ruth gazed down at the pilot sprawled on his back in the bottom of the boat. She talked to him as she rowed. "You're not worth the effort it's costing me to save your life. You lit up my forest, you little prick. I should just let you die. But I won't let Commander Cash down."

Reaching the shore, Ruth beached her little craft, then propped the pilot up. Filling her water bag, she splashed his face with water, and thought she saw his lips move, but his eyes remained closed. As far as she could tell, he was still unconscious. Quickly, Ruth hid the pistol, the briefcase, and the small pouch in the underbrush. She couldn't carry the pilot and all that baggage, too.

Positioning herself beside the boat, Ruth lifted him, draping him across her shoulders just like a fireman, and turned up the trail for home. He was a heavy load, and she stumbled a few times, but then she found a walking rhythm that worked. Her progress was slow and clumsy, with many stops for rests. After a while, she lowered him to the ground and drug him, grasping him under his arm pits.

What had taken her half an hour to walk in, now took over two hours to pack her prisoner out. Sweat was rolling down her face and Ruth was exhausted by the time they reached her tower. With Winnie barking from inside the storeroom, she carried the pilot the last few steps to the wire basket and lowered him into the hamper. With his weight gone, she opened the water bag to wash her face and poured some on her shoulders, which were on fire from carrying the half-dead pilot. She also attempted to give him some water, and this time his lips moved at the taste. She was honestly surprised that he was still alive.

Crossing to the storeroom, she let Winnie out, and the little dog raced for the bushes to do his business. It was getting dark, the shadows lengthening, and she needed to radio the Navy as soon as possible. Returning to the pilot, she tied him into the basket, making him ready for the lift up to her nest. She used short ropes around his legs and torso, with his hands tied together on his lap.

Just as she finished securing her load, she heard a sound, and looked up to find another Jap standing over her, pistol in his hand. He was dressed in a flight suit just like the one her pilot wore. She supposed he was the copilot she had seen parachuting from his plane.

He gestured for her to stand up, his pistol trained on Ruth.

Ruth got to her feet slowly, scared out of her wits.

The man slapped her hard across her face yelling at her in what she supposed must be Japanese. Ruth fell to the ground next to the basket, and he kicked her, pointing his gun at her head. More loud Japanese words.

Barking, Winnie raced towards the intruder.

The man looked away from Ruth and fired at the dog, but he missed, and Winnie ran for cover, while Ruth jammed her whistle between her lips and blew through it with all the breath she had.

Just like the mother bear, the Nip was startled. But he didn't run off. Instead, he turned on her with a look of fury and cocked his pistol again as she struggled to get on her feet.

Pointing at the pilot in the basket, she shouted desperately, "Your friend is alive. He needs a doctor."

The Nip raised his gun, hatred etched on his face.

Ruth frozen in place, was mouthing a silent prayer. Was this the end?

Then something huge came charging out of the shadows an unlikely angel appeared – Mr. Maggot. He pushed himself between Ruth and the copilot, bellowing, "You stay away from my golden mermaid, Zipper Head! She's mine. Hurt her and I'll kill you!"

The Nip pulled the trigger, with a deafening bang.

Shot in the chest, Maggot didn't flinch. Instead, he yelled back at the copilot, "That little pee shooter? I'm bulletproof." Then he tackled the copilot, wrapping both hands around the man's neck.

The two of them fell to the ground, locked together, rolling. Maggot had him by the throat and wasn't letting go. He was shot twice more in the scuffle but not before his massive hands completed their task. In less than a minute, both men were dead, one strangled, the other from three bullet wounds.

Stunned by what she had just witnessed, Ruth couldn't stop shaking. She staggered to her feet and stood, looking down at the two men with tears in her eyes. Maggot had saved her life!

But now what? For some reason she felt guilty for setbacks of the storm, the dangers of the pineapples and now the death of two men. She couldn't just leave their bodies out in the open for predators to maul. So she decided to roll Maggot's body off the copilot and then, remembering how she'd been fooled at the downed plane, checked their pulses to confirm that both men were now just lifeless bodies. She removed the pistol from the copilot's hand and put it in her pocket. Then she covered them up with a canvas tarp from the storeroom using her firewood as weights. And finally, although she was too drained for anything fancy or longwinded, she said a few words of thanks over Maggot's body. He was surely the most unlikely angel she would ever encounter in her life. It was just as Roy had said: *Expect the unexpected.*

With darkness fast approaching, Ruth put aside her emotions and started up the stairs, determined to radio in. She was already half an hour past her deadline, and she needed to speak with Commander Cash. But as she reached the top, she heard a lone wolf howl, out in the woods, and remembered that the pilot was still hog-tied in the basket.

Rushing to the pulley system, Ruth started cranking. By the glow of her flashlight, she watched the hamper slowly creep up the forty-foot tower. Once she had maneuvered it onto the catwalk, she untied the pilot and pulled him inside, placing him on her sleeping bag.

He was so slack that she wasn't sure he was still alive, but when she poured some water into a cup and lifted his head, he managed to drink a little, his chapped lips moving, his eyes still closed.

Warming up the radio, Ruth clicked onto the network. "Cloud Girl reporting in. I need to talk to Commander Cash. Over."

"You're late," a voice answered from the Air Station. "He's on the fire line at Thunder Mountain. Over."

"Then I'll talk to Doctor Wong. Over."

"Sorry, he's on the line, too. Over."

"Then give them this message: 'Cloud Girl reporting in, one dead Jap copilot, one dead escaped convict, and another Jap pilot near death. I need a tower call from Doctor Wong as soon as possible or the second pilot will die. Over and out.'

There was silence for the longest moment. Then the voice answered, "Yes, ma'am! I'll see they get this message ASAP! Over and out."

As she clicked off the radio, the pilot on her bed stirred.

Turning to him, Ruth found his eyes open, staring at her. She brought the cup of water to him, and he drank a little more, his tongue moving weakly across his lips while his black eyes watched her.

"Looks like you might live," she said. "Welcome to my nest. They call me Ruth."

He moved his head slightly, glancing around the room. Ruth propped him up with two of her pillows and washed his face again with a wet cloth. Then she remembered the bottle of whiskey she'd found hidden away behind some books. She retrieved the bottle and gave him a sip.

His eyes opened wider, and he licked his lips again.

"You like whiskey, huh?"

He nodded, moving his left arm and hand.

Had he understood her English question about the whiskey? Was he bilingual or had it been just a coincidence?

She gave him another taste of whiskey and he reached up to hold the cup. There was no more blood coming from his ear and the welt on his temple looked painful.

"What's your name?" Ruth asked.

He pointed at his mouth and shook his head.

"You can't talk?"

He nodded, licking his lips, and moved his hand as if he held a pencil.

"You want to write your name?"

He nodded, and Ruth retrieved her diary book and pencil. She held the pad for him as he used his left hand to scratch out: George Aoki – American born!

## Chapter Fifteen

### Twist of Fate

In the light of one kerosene lamp, Ruth glared at the Nip pilot after reading the words he'd written in her journal. "American born, my ass," she finally said in an angry voice. He looked so unassuming, sprawled on top of her sleeping bag, his face young and fresh. But she knew better.

"Is this some kind of trick? You're in a Jap uniform, flying a Jap plane, and born of Jap blood. Now you want me to believe you're an American citizen? I was born in the morning but not yesterday morning."

Nodding his head, he turned the page of her diary and wrote with difficulty: Hollywood High School, class of 37

Ruth shook her head, frowning. "You've been watching too many American movies, mister. Japanese people don't live in Hollywood, California. Only the rich do."

He wrote more: Father Japanese diplomat, Mother Western Hafu wife.

His eyelids began to droop as he showed her the new message. By the time she managed to decipher his script he had passed out again. Ruth stood and looked down at him. He was breathing better but still had a fever with sweat rolling down his face.

Refreshing her cloth with clean water, she said to Winnie, "I can't trust this guy. How could any American become a Jap pilot, bombing his own homeland?"

Ruth washed the pilot's face again. Then she pulled off his boots and searched the pockets of his tattered flight suit. He had no wallet or other means of identification, not even dog tags like all the American GIs wore.

What would her brother Nick do with this Jap pilot? She shuddered at the thought. The boy would be dead by now.

Ruth found the manual on nursing she had borrowed from Lucy Wilson. She had no idea what to do next for the young aviator. Maybe he'd drop dead, and she would have to put him under the woodpile tarp with Mr. Maggot and the copilot.

Winnie paced the little room, obviously uncomfortable with a stranger in the house. To distract him, Ruth fed him some canned dog food. He was hungry and so was she. Ruth was also worn out from carrying the pilot from the lake, but where was she going to sleep? The Nip could kill her in the middle of the night. And why hadn't she heard back from Doctor Wong?

Lighting the second lamp and closing the drapes, she poured herself some water and ate some beef jerky with a corn biscuit. Then she remembered the copilot's pistol she had stowed in her overalls. With her adrenaline still pumping, she had forgotten all about it. It was the gun used to kill Mr. Maggot. She unloaded the pistol and thought about using it as a club. Instead, she hid the weapon behind the books that concealed the partial pint of whiskey. Hoping to steady her nerves, she took the little bottle out and drank her first mouthful of liquor. It was awful and burnt her throat all the way down to her toes! Why did men drink such firewater?

In her pocket, she also found the gold cross and the picture of the two women that she had taken away from the wreckage. She tucked both items inside the radio manual, for safekeeping, knowing they must be important to the pilot.

Still restless, Ruth put some coffee on the stove to heat, and discovered in doing so that she only had one filled water bag remaining. She would have to return to the lake soon. If the pilot lived through the night, could she leave him alone in her nest while she visited the lake?

She read in the nursing manual how to take the pulse of a sick person, and did so with the pilot. He was still breathing, and she washed his face again while reading more from the manual.

With an eerie red glow still showing in the sky from all the fires, the radio finally came on. "Doctor Wong for Cloud Girl. Got your message. Who are the living and who are the dead? Over."

Ruth quickly replied, "One Nip copilot and one convict laborer are dead. Another near-death patient that survived a plane crash needs your help. Over."

Wong inquired, "What kind of patient and medical condition? Over."

"Male subject, early twenties, bleeding from right ear. The bleeding has stopped for now. He has a golf-ball-sized welt over his ear. Patient in and out of consciousness. Can't or won't talk. He's badly scratched-up with other bruises and lacerations. Over."

"Who is this patient to you? Over." Dr. Wong asked.

"Can't say on the radio, sir," Ruth answered. "Just that he's a pineapple delivery man, sir. Over."

There was a long pause on the doctor's end of the conversation. Finally he responded, "Sounds like a bad concussion, or maybe he's in shock. I'll drop in tomorrow about 8 AM to make a tower call. Meet me at the center of your lake with your boat. For now, give him two Aspirin from your kit and one half of a morphine stick to help him sleep. If the swelling goes down overnight, his voice might return. Keep him as comfortable as you can. Over."

"Bring him some whiskey, sir. He seems to like it. How did you know I have a boat? Over."

"Roy told me he fished from your boat. Over."

Just the mention of Roy's name brought back a flood of fond memories from a few days before. "Are the bridges and roads up to the mountain open yet? Over." Ruth asked.

"No, it will take another couple of days to get to Hebo Butte. The fires are mostly under control, but stay alert. If you see any new flare-ups, report them immediately. Look for me tomorrow morning at the end of a long rope ladder. I'll be the man wearing a life jacket. Over and out."

Knowing that Doctor Wong was coming to help gave her some encouragement, if only the young pilot lived through the night. With Winnie in her arms, she checked her watch. She had a half-hour before her check-in. That was just enough time for her to take the flashlight and visit the storeroom to pick-up an extra sleeping bag and blanket. She would sleep outside on her catwalk for this night.

As her dog took care of his business, Ruth used the outhouse, but found the little room as dark as a coal mine and as spooky as the Wizard of Oz. Sitting on the toilet, she had a sudden memory of Mr. Maggot strangling the copilot. Next, she envisioned how she had shot her pistol at the plane as it flew over her tower. Then came a sweaty recollection of the pilot in her bed, writing out that he was American born! Haunted by those thoughts and more, she finished her business and was outside the storeroom like a bolt of lightning. It had been a horrible day filled with memories she would not soon forget. Her life was dark and hot and she felt as if her world was upside down.

Hands trembling, Ruth returned to her nest and found the pilot still unconscious. She checked his pulse again and moistened his lips with water. Then she warmed up her radio equipment for the check-in with her group. At 9AM sharp, Chief Forester Jacobs was the first to speak. "The Office of Censorship has given us their official news report to be released to the general public." He read the release to them; the Japanese attack on the Tillamook forest was described as ordinary fires started by lighting along with practice fly-overs by three unidentified aircraft on a training mission. There was no mention at all of enemy aircraft. The fires were reported as being 80% contained, with a weather forecast calling for rain in the next forty-eight hours.

No one in the group questioned the lies and half-truths in the report. It was a typical government cover-up for the good of the local population. The last thing the military wanted was hysteria on the home front, and nobody used the word 'pineapple.'

The final comments came from the Chief Forester. "The wind storm hit us hard and we are still trying to get the utilities working and roads open. Don't let your guard down. If you see flare-ups, report them right away. The blimps are a great asset in helping us douse the fires. Over and out."

Ruth poured herself some coffee, thinking hard. When she went out to sleep on the catwalk, should she bring the pistol she had hidden away? Was the pilot any danger to her? She didn't know.

A series of moans came from the sleeping bag, startling her. They were the first noises the pilot had made all night.

She moved her chair next to his bed and wiped his brow again. "You're making sounds. That's good!"

His eyes blinked open and he moved his left arm, pointing to her diary again. He seemed to want to write more, so she held the book for him and guided his shaky hand to the page.

My briefcase, you have it?

"What briefcase?" she answered, remembering the leather pouch she had hidden away.

From plane, he wrote. Need it to prove I'm American born.

"Don't start that again," Ruth said with a frown. "You want some coffee?"

He shook his head. More whiskey? I need my pouch. You must get it.

Ruth stood. "I'll get the whiskey. Then I'll show you what I brought away from your plane."

As she got to her feet the pilot reached out and touched her arm. Then he pointed again to his words: 'you must get it.'

She looked at his desperate face and nodded. "Alright. I have your pouch. It's hidden, down by the lake. I'll get it tomorrow when I pick up the doctor."

Who are you? Where are we? What doctor?

To those written questions, and many more, Ruth replied as the best she could. She reintroduced herself as Ruth Nelson and he wrote out his Japanese name as Lieutenant Aoki. His American name was George Aoki. She showed him the picture of the two women and the golden cross she had removed from his plane. Writing, he explained that the young girl in the kimono was his sister, while the attractive Western lady was Emma Dante Aoki, his Caucasian mother. The gold cross had been given to him by his mother when he was baptized into the Christian faith.

To Ruth, it all seemed so innocent, so family like. How could he be a Jap pilot? She gave him the last of the whiskey, two aspirins, and a half a syringe of morphine to help him sleep.

She talked and he wrote, back and forth, until he dozed off. He called himself a 'Nikkei' a Japanese word she did not understand. It was almost midnight by the time Ruth turned off his lamp and retired to her catwalk, taking along the unloaded pistol, wrapped in the towel she was using as a pillow. She was resolved only to use the gun as a threat, if the pilot caused any trouble.

Under the sky's red glow, Winnie curled up next to her. With a sigh, Ruth asked him, "Why is there so much hate in the world?"

She had a hard time finding dreamland, that night, all too aware that it looked as if hell were just over the next burning horizon. She was frightened, and she questioned the series of decisions that had led to her being trapped in the tower.

At first light, the next morning, Ruth put on the coffee. Then she placed Winnie in the basket and cranked him down to ground level to take care of business. She hadn't slept well. She worried about all the smoldering fires and wondered if there were any new flare-ups. With coffee and binoculars in hand, she walked her catwalk, looking for any new signs of fire but didn't find any.

When she went inside, she put the gun back behind the whiskey and checked on George, he was still deeply asleep. She had to shake him hard to rouse him. "Sorry to wake you but I have to leave soon."

Ever so slowly, his eyes opened, and he made a gurgling sound trying to talk. He looked around the room, shaking his head, an expression of wonderment on his face as if he couldn't recall where he was or what had happened.

"Doctor Wong is coming this morning," Ruth reminded him. "I'll be gone a few hours. Do you want something to eat and drink before I leave? I've got coffee and I can warm up a can of beans."

With a steadier hand than the night before, he wrote

his answer: *coffee, rice and beans?"*

Ruth smiled at him, "Sorry, just beans, no rice. But I do have beef jerky."

He nodded his approval and wrote: *Bedpan?*

Ruth reached under his platform and pulled out the copper pot. "Do you need help? I have a brother, so I know about boys."

George glared at her and shook his head. *I can manage*, he wrote, clearly embarrassed.

Ruth took his pulse and looked closely at the welt above his ear. "Your lump looks better. Doctor Wong will know what to do next. He's the Flight Surgeon for all the American pilots around here," Ruth told him.

He wrote out: *Is he Chinese? They hate all Japanese people. He will kill me!*

Ruth was caught off guard by his comment. "No! He won't kill you. He is an honorable man, one who volunteered to come all the way out here to save your life."

*He will kill all Japanese people!* He wrote, and pointed at his words for emphasis.

Ruth felt anger well inside of her. "I didn't carry you all the way up here just to see you die," she protested. "Yesterday, I watched two men kill each other. It was a sad and tragic event to witness. There will be no more talk of deaths in my fire-tower. The war is over for you."

Ruth fed George and gave him some coffee. "I'll bring your briefcase when I come back. Stay in bed and rest."

George nodded, looking sad, and wrote: *You*

*carried me here?*

"Yes, on my back," Ruth answered. "And now Dr. Wong is coming here to fix you up."

*Why did you save me?*

"Because you needed saving. Anyhow, that's what Christians do."

With Winnie in the lead and Ruth carrying three empty water bags, they headed for the lake. The morning was cloudy with just a gentle breeze. That was good, and the lack of fog was even better. The blimp would have a clear view as it hovered over the lake.

Walking the trail, Ruth found herself reliving the happenings of the day before. There was so much anger in the local communities for anything Japanese that she feared for the pilot's safety. If the local citizens ever got hold of him, he'd be lynched in a heartbeat. The Chinese were at war with the Japanese, who were at war with the Americans, and all for what? Scrap iron, coal, oil... who cared? People were dying.

Upon their arrival at the lake, Ruth saw steam rolling off the water in the cool morning air. She uncovered her boat and checked her watch. She was early, with no signs of a blimp in the sky. Carefully, she removed George's briefcase and the other smaller map pouch from underneath the boat and examined them again. The smaller pouch held only a few maps and Japanese documents she could not read. The briefcase was filled with other documents on folded blue paper that smelled of ammonia. Upon inspection they looked like some kind of plans for a boat. In the bottom of the briefcase, she found an American passport issued to George Aoki in 1937, with his picture. She also found a small metal canister, the kind that usually held thirty-five mm film. These items and the film might be the proof he needed to show that he was American born. Could she trust him now?

Leaving Winnie on the shore, Ruth took both pouches with her as she dragged the skiff to the lake and paddled off. Doctor Wong would know what to do with the pilot's items. For now, her mission was to get the good doctor safely into her boat.

Checking her watch again, she paddled out to deep water and rowed around the wreckage of the plane one more time, waiting for the blimp. The lake was calm, but the steam rolling off the water made a gray and ominous landscape. There were oil streaks coming from the plane's engine, and other debris floating around the wreckage. Viewing it by the light of day, Ruth was all the more surprised that George had lived through such a crash.

She heard the soft purring of the blimp before she could see it. Looking skyward through the steam a few moments later, she spotted it just above the tree tops. The dirigible was slowly moving from the north to the south at an altitude of about two hundred fifty feet, casting its giant shadow across the water of the lake.

Ruth rowed as fast as she could to get under the belly of the blimp. When she reached a spot under the gondola, the blimp stopped moving. Looking up at it reminded Ruth of watching a fictional aluminum space craft from the movies. It just hovered over her for the longest time. Then one of the doors of the gondola opened. A sailor waved down at her, then pushed out a canvas bag tied to a rope. “Take these supplies first,” the sailor shouted through a voice horn. “Doc Wong will be next.”

As soon as Ruth succeeded in manhandling the bag into her boat and untying the line, the rope was pulled back up and into the blimp. The next item out the door was a rope ladder… but it stopped unfurling well above her boat.

“You need to come down about twenty feet,” Ruth shouted up at the blimp.

Next out of the gondola was Doctor Wong, wearing a yellow lifejacket. With his back to the open door, he started down the rope ladder, one shaky step at a time. He didn’t look down, just slowly moved from one rung to the next. But a sudden gust of wind moved the blimp up instead of down, and it set the rope ladder swinging like a pendulum.

From the shore, Winnie started barking, running up and down on the beach while he eyed the strange goings-on.

“Down, not up,” Ruth shouted to the sailor.

He waved back at her. “We’re having turbulence from the fires, up here.”

Finally, the blimp answered her helm and dropped down about twenty feet with a quick jerk. The bottom of the rope ladder finally was in the water, and Doc Wong scurried down another twenty feet, but the blimp started to move up again. He shouted at her, “I’m jumping in. Pick me up in the water.”

Then he let go of the rope ladder and fell about fifteen feet into the lake with a loud splash.

Ruth paddled to him and helped him climb into the skiff, the maneuver almost capsizing her boat. Once the doctor was safely aboard, Ruth gave him a welcoming smile. "Cloud Girl reporting for duty, sir."

I don't know why I volunteered for this mission," he replied, taking off his wet lifejacket. "I don't even know how to swim."

They both waved up at the sailor who still stood at the open door of gondola. "My regards to the Captain. We'll make it safely ashore," the doc shouted to the sailor as the electric engines started again. Within a few moments the blimp, like a giant silver bird, was flying high above tree tops, heading south once again.

# Chapter Sixteen

## Dr. Wong

Ruth had only talked personally to Doctor Wong a few times but she had heard quite a bit about him. It was said that he came from a rich Chinese family that still lived in Hong Kong. The scuttlebutt was that his grandfather, a humble foot doctor, had once saved the life of a famous American admiral during the Boxer Rebellion of 1901. His act of humanity had sealed a special bond between the US Navy and the Wong family. During the First World War, his father, Dr. Lee Wong, had been the first Chinese physician allowed to join the Navy as a ship's doctor. Now Dr. Lee's son was the first Chinese flight surgeon in the Navy. There were deep ties between these two parties and some believed it had to do with the very future of the Mandarin Empire itself. Doc Wong spoke and read over twenty different languages and dialects. He was considered by most as a mystery man of high integrity and personal intellect. All Ruth knew for certain was that he was one smart man!

She studied his face with curiosity. He looked young, maybe in his early thirties, a soft-spoken man with honey-colored skin and deep brown eyes that were set at a slant.

He stood up cautiously in the skiff, taking off his trousers and shirt. Then, settling himself, he began wringing out his garments.

It seemed to be of no concern to him that he was only wearing his underwear in front of Ruth. "Alright, young lady," he said, "I'm here. Tell me about this secret patient of yours. What makes this guy so special?"

Ruth paddled for the sunny side of the lake, to help dry out the Doc's clothes. As they passed by the wreckage, she asked, "What would you say if I told you that an American pilot was flying that wreckage over there?

"Impossible," Dr. Wong answered, squeezing water out of his socks. "That's definitely a Jap seaplane. No American would know how to fly such a craft."

Ruth opened George's briefcase and handed over the passport, "George Aoki is the pilot's name. He was certified as an American citizen in 1937. And he was definitely the pilot, Doc. I shot at his plane when he flew it over my nest. He crashed here on the lake and lived through it, so I carried him back to my tower yesterday. He's still alive, but just barely. That's my mystery patient."

Dr. Wong considered the information. "What happened to his copilot?"

"Like I told you yesterday, he's dead, along with an escaped convict from the County Farm. They killed each other in hand-to-hand combat. There was nothing I could do about it, sir."

The doctor smiled at her. "You've done a lot, Ruthie. May I call you Ruthie? You shot down an enemy plane and captured its pilot. If you do that five more times, they'll call you an Air Ace. I'd say you're one heroic Firewatcher."

"You can call me, Ruthie sir. But I didn't shoot him down. I just shot *at* his plane."

As they floated in the sunshine, Ruth showed the doctor George's briefcase. He was amazed with the contents. He could read Japanese, and explained to her what some of the documents were about. He seemed most excited by the blueprints, which he said were of a new type of boat that the Japs were calling the I-400-class submarine. Those underwater aircraft carriers could launch and recover three seaplanes per boat, any place in the world.

"I'm no expert on submarines," the doc said, looking over the blueprints, "but I'll bet my bottom dollar the planes that attacked our forest came from the decks of one these new subs. This is hot stuff, Ruthie. We've got to get this information to Navy Intelligence."

"That's why I needed you here, sir. I had no idea what to do next, with him *or* with his pouches."

With the doctor's clothes almost dry, Ruth rowed for shore and asked him what was in his supply bag. He told her it contained two doctor bags, one for traditional Western medicine and the other for Asian medicine. "If our patient is Japanese, he'll more than likely prefer the Asian. But if the size of his welt isn't improving, I may need my traditional bag to drain fluid off his brain. That could be a tricky, so I remembered to bring the whiskey."

When they got to shore, Ruth showed Dr. Wong the

shoulder holster and gun she had removed from the plane.

"Yesterday, I didn't know what to do with the pistol, so I just hid it here in the brush. Should we take it back to the tower?"

As the doctor pulled on his damp clothes, he replied, "I hate guns, but yes, I'll wear the holster. Your pilot is still the enemy, until we can prove otherwise."

Ruth filled the water bags and put the two leather pouches inside the doctor's supply bag. She would carry the water and he would carry the supplies. Then she hid the boat again, upside down, and covered it with tree branches.

As they moved down the trail, Dr. Wong said, "You were an amazingly brave girl, pulling that pilot out of his plane. He could have killed you." Then he expressed his amazement that she had carried the pilot on her back. "He had to outweigh you. How did you do that?"

"Fireman style," Ruth answered. "I watched some volunteer fireman training at our firehouse. It's all about balancing the weight."

Ruth turned to the doctor with a sheepish face, "I dropped him a few times, on the trail. I didn't mean to. I just did."

As they moved along, Ruth kept a keen eye on her watch for the 9AM check-in. When they got back to the tower, she showed Dr. Wong the two dead bodies under the firewood weighted tarp.

He looked at them carefully, then covered them up again. "As soon as the roads open, we'll send them down the mountain to the County Morgue. They will know what to do."

When they had loaded the wire basket with the water and supplies Ruth and the doc walked up the stairs to her nest. Reaching the catwalk, Ruth pointed out her view of the surrounding forests, and the doctor seemed deeply taken with the breathtaking landscape.

Inside the hut, Ruth warmed up her radio, then went back out to crank up the basket. When the cargo arrived on the catwalk, Dr. Wong removed one of his medical bags. "I'll go in and examine the pilot."

Once she had unloaded the rest of the cargo from the basket, she headed inside to await her radio check-in, only to be greeted by the sound of George Aoki saying, "I'll kill you if you touch me."

"Cloud Girl, we have a problem here," Dr. Wong said, his voice choking with tension. "George has a gun pointing at me."

Ruth moved immediately to her bed platform, scowling. "George, I told you this morning no more talk of deaths in my tower. Dr. Wong is here to help you, not kill you."

With the copilot's gun pointing unsteadily at Dr. Wong, George rasped, "He's wearing my gun. I want it back."

Ruth stepped directly in front of the doctor, blocking him from the pointed gun. "Are you going to shoot me, George? I saved your life and now you're going to kill me?"

George shook his head. "No, I trust you, girl. I'll only kill the Chinaman."

"You want your pistol back? Okay, I'll trade it for the gun you're holding. Deal?"

"All right," George said, "I'll trade."

"Good." Ruth turned to Dr. Wong. "Hand him your pistol."

Stone-faced, the doctor unsnapped the shoulder holster and handed the pistol to George. George, in turn, handed his gun to Ruth. There was a palpable tension in the room, with everyone waiting to see what would happen next. Then the radio crackled to life for the check-in.

Ruth held up her gun. "Now we both have the same thing – empty guns. I threw away my bullets, last night, and the doc threw away his bullets, this morning at the lake. So we both have the same thing again: empty guns!"

With a frown, George opened the breech of his gun and confirmed that it was empty. Ruth did the same. "George, let the doctor examine you. It's time for you to live, not die."

Calm and collected, Ruth returned to her radio and checked in with her group, saying absolutely nothing about her two visitors and the gun battle she had just disarmed.

As Dr. Wong examined George, he began to speak in Japanese to him and saw that the young pilot seemed impressed that he knew the language. The doctor carefully poked and prodded him, cleaning the lacerations and bruises.

Across the room, Ruth concluded her check-in and said, "I can't understand a word you guys are saying. What's the medical report, Doc?"

"What can I say? He's young, strong. Over all, he's in much better shape than I first feared," the doc answered. Palpating the welt, he said, "I'm going to drain this lump now and I'll need your help. Get my Asian bag and some hot water and clean cloths. Then help me to hold him steady as I lance his welt."

The doctor's Asian bag was filled with roots and herbs in small glass jars labeled with Chinese markings. Dr. Wong selected a jar and held it up. "Dried Mongolia mushrooms," he announced, and cut off the stem of a single black mushroom. "Chew on this," he told George. "It will make you sleep while I drain your welt. When you wake up, you should be able to speak better."

George nodded and chewed the mushroom stem, making a sour face. Within minutes, he was sleeping.

"Here, Ruth, come close. Hold his shoulders down in case he rouses," the doctor instructed, then used a syringe to suck out clear fluid from around the welt. "There. That should relieve some of the pressure on his brain. Thanks for your help. You did just fine." He smiled. "I noticed you had a nurse's manual in your bookcase. Have you considered becoming a nurse?"

Cleaning the welt with hot water, Ruth replied, "That might be nice, but my family needs me around the farm. I borrowed the book from a girlfriend." She shrugged. "Maybe someday I'll go to nursing school."

With George still asleep and the dog pacing the room, Dr. Wong and Ruth continued their talk. "I was thinking about you this morning," the doctor said, "and all that you have accomplished as a Firewatcher. That was a gutsy move, to stand in front of his pistol this morning. I'm impressed with your grit. You're the only girl I've ever known who has shot down an airplane. You're going to be a hero by the time this is over."

"I'm no hero," Ruth said. "The heroes are the fire

fighters. I was only doing my job. What we need now is to know more about George Aoki and what's in his briefcase. How did he get here: and why the Tillamook Forest?"

"Yes." Dr. Wong said closing up his medical bags. "When he wakes up, we'll use a little whiskey to loosen his lips. This boy has a story that needs to be told."

Ruth let the dog out and put on a fresh pot of coffee. By then, it was time for one of her fire patrols, and she walked her perch with coffee and binoculars in hand. Thunderclouds were building in the east, so she made notes about the weather and reported one small aircraft landing at the Air Station. Using the glasses, she could only see two fires still smoldering in the forest between Hebo Butte and Buzzard Butte, and both looked to be under control. Only the Thunder Mountain fire seemed to be actively burning. She needed to check it out. But as she turned for her hut, Dr. Wong walked out onto her catwalk. "I owe you an apology," he said, handing her an envelope. "With all the excitement of dropping in via the blimp, I forgot that Roy gave me this letter for you."

Ruth beamed as she took the envelope and put it in her pocket. "Thank you, I'll read it later. Right now, I'm going to ride my bike up to the summit of Hebo Mountain where I'll have a better view of the Thunder Mountain fire. Help yourself to any food or coffee while I'm gone. If I can get by the blown-down trees, I'll be back in couple hours."

"You're a little sweet on Deputy Roy aren't you?" the doctor asked.

"We're good friends," Ruth answered with a slight blush. "I hope to see him soon."

As soon as Ruth had ridden her bike up the road, just out of sight, she stopped to read Roy's letter. The entire Sheriff's Office and Fire Department had been on call, ever since the wind storm. Nearly every able-bodied person in the County had been fighting the fires or repairing the roads. Roy wrote of long, hot days and short, cool nights, building bridges and opening roads. He had heard that Mr. Maggot had been killed in an accident and wanted more details.

Ruth frowned; another Government cover-up she couldn't talk about.

*I often think of you and the meal we shared together,* Roy wrote. I *heard of a new kind of kiss we should try. It's called the Italian smooch. It sounds like fun, so keep my whistle around your neck and use it when you need me. See you soon, sweet Ruth. XOXO, Roy.*

It wasn't much of a romantic letter, but then the past few days hadn't been much of a romantic time. "Expect the unexpected," she said out loud to Winnie, and they moved farther up the road.

A few hours later, Ruth and Winnie returned to the tower and found George sitting-up in his bed, his briefcase open, and papers scattered around the room. Next to his platform was the open bottle of whiskey the doctor had brought along, a bottle that was now nearly half empty!

Dr. Wong was on the radio, talking to someone at the Air Station. "Tell Commander Cash I'm awaiting his instructions. Have him contact me on this frequency. This is a Priority One message. Over and out."

He looked up from the radio and greeted Ruth with a big smile. “I’ve spent most of my morning on the radio, talking with the Twelfth Naval District in Seattle. We’re trying to figure out what to do with George. He and I are getting along just fine, and his fever is way down. In fact, he’s made a remarkable improvement, considering all he’s been through. He likes my whiskey and he has a fantastic story to tell. Pull up a chair and join us. I’ll fill you in.”

Having two men in her tiny nest was uncomfortable for Ruth. She felt as if the walls to her hut were constantly shrinking inward.

## Chapter Seventeen

**George Aoki**

George's voice was stronger, and his eyes brighter. Relieved, Ruth joined the men, who were talking like chatterboxes about baseball, war, and the weather. While the pilot's American name was George Aoki, his Japanese name was Kai Aoki.

"He's one-hundred-percent Yankee born!" Dr. Wong said to her. "Saint Francis Hospital in San Francisco on August 15th, 1918."

His father Harorudo Aoki, (American name, Harold), had come to America as a low-level diplomat during the First World War and worked for a time at the Japanese Embassy in Washington D.C. He was then promoted to a position as an Agricultural Trade Represent-tative and transferred to California in 1921. There he met and married his beautiful wife of Italian descent, Emma Dante, in San Francisco. She was a lounge singer and Harold soon became her most devoted fan.

The couple had two children, a boy and a girl. George was the oldest. The family purchased an orange grove in Encino California in 1928, just before the Great Depression. They struggled with the groves for the first few years but then, thanks to Harold's contacts back in Japan and his wife's golden voice in the many Hollywood speakeasies, they flourished. Harold and Emma Aoki were an ideal American family, living out their dreams on sixty acres of some of the best orange groves in California. They had money and influence, and their children were well educated.

In his junior year at Hollywood High School, George Aoki fell in love with flying. He took lessons, day and night, at the Santa Monica airport. By his sixteenth birthday, he was the first teen-aged pilot to be licensed to fly both single-and double-engine aircraft. George gained a reputation as a 'born flyer.' In the summers, he even worked on the flight line, and soon became a certified aircraft mechanic.

Then, in July of 1937, the Second Sino-Japanese War began. The Japanese Government immediately recalled nearly all their diplomatic missions worldwide, including Harold Aoki, but not including his Caucasian wife Emma or their American born children. Most of the Japanese-Americans living on the US west coast at the time didn't want to return to their homeland. However, if they refused to return, they knew that their relatives back in Japan would face retribution. As a result, after living almost twenty years in America, Harold Aoki signed over his share of the orange groves to Emma and his son and daughter. He then boarded a ship for Japan. Little did he or anyone else know the bleak future that lay ahead for the Aoki family.

Upon his return to Japan, Harold found the ruthless wartime government more regimented then he remembered from his youth in Tokyo. Politicians had outlawed all mixed marriages and no longer recognized the children of these unions. Harold lobbied the government to bring his family over to Japan but the request was refused. Then a warmonger bureaucrat found out about Harold's son, the pilot, back in the US, and the Government agreed to allow the son to come for a visit.

That was the summer of 1938. Once George set foot in Japan, the Japanese Government refused to let him go. Within a few weeks of his arrival, he was drafted into the Japanese Navy as a flight instructor, while his father was stripped of his duties and sent to a political prison for reeducation, or what became commonly known as 'brain washing.' As a result, an American citizen was forced to teach the Japanese how to fly seaplanes, that flew with mostly American-built engines! But with his father's reputation and life in the balance, George could not complain, and undertook his assigned military activities patriotically.

"That's when I first heard about the I-400 project," George said, sipping his whiskey and holding up the blueprints. "Just imagine eighteen of these submarines with three aircraft per boat. That's thirty-six aircraft that could attack anywhere in the world."

"They have eighteen I-400 submarines?" Ruth asked.

"No," George assured her. "But the government has ordered eighteen to be delivered by the spring of 1944. I flew here from the deck of the prototype, which was launched just a few months ago at the Hiroshima shipyards."

"Why did you target our forest?" Dr. Wong asked.

"That's their plan for the summer of '44. With a few dozen Japanese planes and a thousand FU GO bombs, there could be one giant wildfire burning from the California state line to the Canadian border. America must stop Tojo from building those submarines. That's why I promised my father that I would undertake this mission. America needs to know about this threat."

"Is your father still in prison?" Ruth asked.

"No, sadly he's dead. After Pearl Harbor, he was executed by a firing squad for trying to smuggle out messages to our family back in the States. Before he died, he begged me to escape and free our family from the internment camp at Tule Lake California. So that's my mission – to exchange wartime secrets for the freedom of my family."

"You can't blackmail the US government," Wong replied.

"I won't. I intend to give them my briefcase freely, with no conditions attached." He opened his case and brought out the small metal film can. "But I give this film canister to Ruth, the Cloud Girl who saved my life, on the sole condition that she will keep it safe until the government releases my family from the internment camp and returns our wrongly confiscated orange groves in Encino. Then she can give the film to the US Navy."

Ruth took the can in hand. "What's so important about these pictures?"

"I took them at the Hiroshima Shipyard. Since I was an expert on Japanese seaplanes, the Navy gave me free access to where the prototype submarine was being built. These are my photographs, inside and out, of the first I-400 boat. The American Nautical Engineers will drool over these pictures."

"So you planned this mission out, all on your own?" Ruth asked.

"No," George answered shaking his head. "It was pure, dumb luck. On the day that the prototype was launched, I overheard two admirals talking about sending the boat on a shakedown cruise to the west coast of America to start forest fires. That's when I jumped at the chance to be back on American soil again."

"So you planned to crash your plane, if need be?" Dr. Wong asked.

"Yes. I was going to land my plane on the lake and surrender. When I told my copilot I was surrendering, he bailed out. He wanted nothing to do with surrendering."

"So that's it? These are your terms?" Dr. Wong asked, coffee cup in hand.

"Yes. But please understand that my name and mission must not be made public. I want the Japanese to think my copilot and I both died in action in your forest. If they think I'm still alive, they will likely kill my relatives who are still living in Japan. This has to be top secret."

Dr. Wong moved to the radio equipment. "Fine. I'll contact the Air Station again and get the ball rolling, and I'll call Admiral King's adjutant about your terms. By this time tomorrow, you could be with your mother and sister at Tule Lake, and then on to your home in Encino."

# Chapter Eighteen

**White Lies**

George nodded his head and slowly stood up, holding onto the bed platform. "I need to use the commode."

"Do you want me to crank you down or walk you down the stairs?" Ruth asked stretching her body from sitting to long on the folding chair.

"I'm in no hurry," George answered.

"Good," she said. "My nest smells like a locker-room with dirty socks, sweat and whiskey. I have to collect the laundry and open up the windows. Then we'll go down the stairs."

Ruth did just that, and rolled up her sleeping bag from the night before. Then, with binoculars in hand, she walked the catwalk again, with George watching her every step.

"Did you see me shoot at your plane when you flew over my tower?" she asked.

George chuckled. "Definitely. One of your bullets whizzed by my ear."

"I'm glad I missed you, George. My boyfriend only gave me one lesson with the pistols."

Standing by the top railing, Ruth smiled back at

him, "I thought I missed you by a mile. Sorry for the close call."

With a small duffle bag of dirty clothes, they slowly descended the flight of stairs. George was wobbly but determined. Once on ground level, they walked around the tower to the storeroom. Along the way, Ruth stopped at the wood covered tarp and rolled it back for George to see. "Here's your copilot, resting next Mr. Maggot, one of our local convict laborers. Your guy shot my guy three times while Mr. Maggot was breaking his neck like a twig. There was nothing I could do about it but watch."

George shook his head. "His name was Lieutenant Fudo. He wholeheartedly believed in the boy emperor Hirohito. He hated Americans and all we stand for. I'm not surprised he's dead."

Ruth covered up the insect-infested bodies with the tarp and replaced the firewood on top. The bodies smelled like death. It was an odor she had never smelled before and she didn't like it one little bit.

Ruth showed George the inside of the storeroom and opened the door to the dark privy. "It's not fancy but it works."

George nodded and turned for the little room.

"Take your time. I forgot my bathrobe so I have to go back up and get it. When you're done in the privy, stay in the storeroom and keep the door locked until I return."

"Why?" he shouted through the door.

"I live in forest full of wild animals."

Returning to the level courtyard that separated the storeroom from the tower, Ruth decided to yell up to Dr. Wong and ask him to throw down her bathrobe. She yelled to him several times but he didn't respond, so she lifted the whistle that hung around her neck blew it hard.

There was still no response from the doctor, but Ruth heard two whistles echo back from the woods. Someone else was out there, but who?

She whistled again, and more echoes answered back. Who could it be?

Finally, Dr. Wong appeared on the catwalk, looking down at Ruth. "Did you whistle for me? I was on the radio with Admiral King's adjutant. They've agreed to George's terms."

"Great news!" Ruth shouted back. "And could you throw down my terrycloth bathrobe? George has been using it as a pillow. I need to wash it."

The doc smiled and disappeared into her hut. Moments later, he reappeared and dropped the bathrobe down to her. "I have more good news," he said. "The bridges leading up the mountain have been repaired, and the road should be open in a couple of hours. The County Coroner is on his way, and so is the Chief Forester. We'll need to get George cleaned up for his trip to Tule Lake."

Ruth gave him a thumbs-up and picked up her robe. "In that case, I'll have him give me his flight suit and I'll wash it, as well."

Returning to the storeroom, she told George the news. As they talked, he confided that he would like to take a bath to get properly cleaned up for his trip. That morning, Ruth had returned with three filled water bags. Now she decided to use all of that water for George's bath. Her clothes would have to wait.

George helped her, as best he could, carry the rubber tub outside and pour all the water into it. Then, as she searched in the storeroom for the bath salts her mother had given her, George undressed down to his skivvies and stepped into the tub. A bath was such a luxury that Ruth wished it was for her enjoyment: the sun, the water and the view. How relaxing!

But that all came to end when Ruth walked out of the storeroom with the salts and saw a gray wolf circling the log-covered tarp of the two dead men. The wolf sniffed the air, showing his fangs. With drool dripping from his snout, the gray was twenty or thirty feet away from them, standing on the lumpy tarp.

George hadn't noticed the wolf yet. Ruth slowly poured the salts into his water. And said, "Don't look up and don't move! There's a wolf standing on the dead bodies. He's watching us. I'm going to slowly reach for my whistle and, *if* I blow it, you and I are going to run for the storeroom and slam the door behind us. Do you understand?"

George moved his head ever so slightly, just enough to make sidelong eye contact with the Gray. "You think you're going to whistle away a wolf?"

"Not likely, but I might be able to scare him a little and make him think twice. I have a knife in my pocket, and I'll grab it before I whistle. Are you ready?"

"No," George answered firmly. "I can't get out of this damn tub or run fast."

"I'll push the tub over and you'll slip right out."

A dog howled in the distance, and the wolf started sniffing the dead men again and scratching at the tarp. Then a whistle blew, but not Ruth's whistle. Lifting its head with a jerk, the wolf started to run away, then stopped and looked back at Ruth and George.

*Bang!*

A gun shot rang out, killing the Gray instantly.

Ruth ran over to the Gray, eyeing the dead animal before a new sound made her raise her gaze. Just down the road, a horse and rider were galloping her way: Deputy Roy Adams, along with his guard-dog, Fang.

In a cloud of dust, Roy pulled his horse to a halt, close to where Ruth still stood by the dead wolf. "Not a bad shot from horseback," he said with a grin. "I heard your whistle down the trail and got here as fast as I could. I've been chasing that damn wolf all morning. It killed one of Mr. Wilson's calves last night, and he put a $50 bounty on its nose and loaned me his plow horse." Then he looked past her at the courtyard and his eyes widened, with a curious face. "What's going on here, Ruthie? Who's that naked man in your bath tub? And what's that god-awful smell?"

Ruth shrugged, trying to keep a straight face. "That's just George. He dropped in for a bath."

"Is he Chinese, like Dr. Wong?"

"No, he's a Japanese-American on his way home."

"Uh-huh" Roy said suspiciously. "And that smell! What is it?"

Ruth shook her head. "Just a couple dead bodies."

"What!"

"Yep, it's Mr. Maggot and a Jap pilot that dropped in. They killed each other. Don't worry. The coroner is on his way to pick up the bodies."

Roy dismounted and walked over to the tarp, holding his nose. "You've been a busy girl, Ruth. Now tell me the truth of it."

She smiled at Roy. "I just did. By the way, nice to see you again, Roy. Dr. Wong is up in my nest, if you need more information. I'm not allowed to say much else about it. Besides, I have to finish getting George cleaned up for his trip."

Taking the hint, Roy walked his horse to the tower steps and tied him to the railing. Then he climbed the stairs, his head full of questions. Something was dreadfully wrong here, and he would demand that Dr. Wong tell him what was going on. After all, he was a Deputy Sheriff. He needed to know these things, and so far two dead bodies and a naked man were all the clues he had!

An hour later, Roy loaded up the dead carcass of the wolf and remounted his horse. He hadn't learned much from Dr. Wong except that like the pineapples this story was classified. He was however, happy to learn there was going to be a small celebration of the reopening of Hebo Butte at 5 o'clock, with just the Firewatcher team and a few others invited.

As Roy turned his horse to leave, George approached him, dressed in his flight suit and clearly feeling better. "Would you be the boyfriend of Ruth?"

"Yes, I guess so." Roy answered. "Where is she?"

"She went to the lake for more water. You're a lucky man, sir. She saved my life and restored my faith in mankind. God bless you both."

Roy looked at him, still confused. "Thank you for your kind words, sir. She is indeed a special girl."

It was late afternoon when Ruth returned from the lake. She was pleased to find that the County Coroner had arrived with his wagon. As the dead men were being carried away, Ruth answered a few questions that the Corner needed for the death certificates. As they drove off, she said a silent farewell to Mr. Maggot. He had taught her the difference between real fear and assumed fear. The mind could play strange tricks with fear. And, in the end, Mr. Maggot had acted bravely and saved her life.

As Ruth was finishing up with the mortician, Roy returned in his Studebaker pickup with Margaret Smith and Hank Johnson riding with him in the cab. In the back of the truck were folding tables, chairs, and ice boxes filled with bottles of beer and sodas.

From down the road came Chief Forester Jacobs in his truck, with Henry Hoyt and Silver Cloud. They brought the real treat, a crab feed compliments of the Hebo Café. And following behind the Forester's truck was Ruth's father, Oscar, and her mother, Helen, in their beat-up old truck.

Just as the party was getting started, Commander Cash from the Air Station drove in with two Shore Patrolmen in his staff car. They pulled up to the tower and honked their horn. Moments later, Dr. Wong and George, disguised in a hooded jacket, came down the stairs and climbed in the car. Without saying a word, they drove away with all the party goers wondering who was that stranger? Why had he needed a Shore Patrol escort? They all looked to Ruth for an explanation, but she was tight-lipped and playing dumb.

Over seafood and beers, the party got going, with all the Firewatchers exchanging stories about the wind storm and the fires. It was a time of friendship that would not be soon forgotten. Oscar even confessed that he had come to like Roy, and respected him as a Deputy Sheriff. "We worked side by side, opening the roads," he confided to Ruth. "The man knows how to work, and I give you my blessing if you want to court him."

Then Helen gave Ruth a surprise gift: a chocolate cake with "Happy 16th Birthday" written in icing on top.

Ruth blinked, startled to find everyone watching her. Then it dawned on her that this was July 20th, her birthday! She had forgotten all about it.

Roy glared at her and said with frustration rolling off his lips, "You told me you were seventeen years old!"

All the Firewatchers chuckled.

"Well," Ruth replied with a smile, "at least no one can call me *jailbait* anymore."

Roy shook his head with a grudging grin. "What the hell am I going to do with you?"

On tiptoe, Ruth kissed him on his lips, right in front of everyone, making Roy blush. "Like pineapples from the sky," she said with a grin, "expect the unexpected!"

***** END *****

# Epilogue

## Firewatcher Epilogue

Small towns have big ears and sharp eyes. The government did its best, writing half-true news stories about the Tillamook Forest without mentioning the real happenings of the Japanese attack, the incendiary pineapples, or the two dead men in the forest.

The locals were wise to their white-washed stories and trusted their own rumor mill. One rumor had it that Ruth had shot down a Japanese plane and rescued an American pilot lost in the forest. Another story boasted that she had killed two downed Nip pilots with their own pistols. Another tidbit claimed she had saved the life of an American pilot, and that he was rescued from the forest by a blimp. These half-true rumors were no more reliable than the government stories. Meanwhile, Ruth and everyone else involved in the Firewatch program remained mum about the attack and the events in and around Hebo Butte on July 20th, 1942. They were sworn to secrecy and they kept that trust sacred.

After her birthday party, Ruth's life went back to normal in her lookout tower as she walked her walk with keen eyes trained on the horizon. The dog days of August were still hot and the forest was still kindle dry. This was the likely time for wildfires, and Ruth was determined to be the first to respond to any such events.

A few Fridays later, Chief Forester Jacobs showed up for his normal resupply trip. Before they began their work, he and Ruth had coffee together. That was when he handed her the small envelope that would change the course of her life. The envelope was formal-looking, neatly typewritten on US Navy stationery, addressed to Ruth Ann Nelson, Oscar Nelson, Helen Nelson, and Officer Roy Adams.

The message inside the envelope was all business as well: 'The US Navy hereby requests your presence at the office of Commander Cash on August 15th, 1942, at the Tillamook Air Station, 17:00 hours. Dress Class A. Please confirm your attendance to Chief Forester Jacobs and allow three hours for said meeting. Signed: Commander Cash, Tillamook Naval Air Station.'

Ruth stared at the message and read it twice, a lump rising in her throat. Why would Commander Cash request such a meeting? And why the inclusion of her parents and Roy? Had they found out that Roy had spent the night, or that she had lied on her application to become a Fire-watcher?

Hesitant, she tried to get out of the meeting. "I don't think it's a good idea for me to be away from my watch," she told the Chief, shaking her head.

"Don't worry about it, Ruthie," he replied. "I'm covering your watch this weekend. Your folks and Roy have already confirmed their attendance. I'll drive you down to your house after we unload the supplies."

"No, please, let my folks and Roy go. That's enough. I'll stay here with my tower."

The Chief glared at her. "Commander Cash 'requested' your presence. In Navy talk, that's a direct order. You have no options. You're going."

Ruth could see no way of getting out of it. With a sigh, she asked, "What does dress 'Class A' mean?"

The Chief smiled at her. "Men in uniform, women wearing a dress. No overalls."

The next evening, the Nelson family all piled into Roy's pickup with Helen sitting on Oscar's lap, Ruth in the middle, and Roy at the wheel. They were all dressed in their Sunday best, with Ruth wearing her graduation dress. She didn't like it but she didn't complain. Everyone was curious about the summons from the Navy. It was like getting a letter from the IRS.

When they got to the front gate, they were directed to the Officers Club. Upon arrival at the club, they were shown into the private dining room of Commander Cash. Once inside, they found the Commander and Dr. Wong waiting there, dressed in their white summer uniforms with rows of colorful battle ribbons on their chest. They were seated at a large dining table, with two white-shirted Filipinos stewards serving refreshments. The Nelsons and Roy were invited to join the officers at the table. It all seemed very friendly and casual, not at all what Ruth had expected.

Once they were all settled with refreshments in hand, Dr. Wong welcomed them and thanked them for coming. Then he started talking about the reasons for their summons.

"As I'm sure you all know, there are wild rumors circulating in town about what happened at Hebo Butte. The rumors are not truthful, so Commander Cash and I would like to set the record straight. *But* be aware that most of the events at Hebo Butte are now classified as Top Secret." Dr. Wong focused on Oscar and Helen. "Still, we can tell you this much – the US Navy and the American Government are deeply grateful for the actions taken by your daughter Ruth. What she did may have changed the course of the war in the Pacific Theater."

"What actions?" Oscar asked, wide-eyed.

"That we can't tell you, sir," Commander Cash replied. "But if Ruth was in the military, she would be awarded the Navy Cross for her bravery and the actions she undertook against the Japanese Government."

Oscar and Helen stared, clearly startled by Dr. Wong's news.

"What kind of bravery?" Roy asked.

"She can't say. Ruth is sworn to secrecy and so are we," Dr. Wong answered. "And so, with our lips sealed, we believe it would be in Ruthie's best interests if she volunteered and joined the Navy."

The room went silent for a moment as the Nelson family looked at each other in astonishment. How could this be? Ruth in the military, she's just little girl!

Commander Cash continued, "We are indebted to Ruth Ann, and have taken the liberty of writing her letters of recommendation to the 12th Naval District. They, in turn, have approved her application to become a cadet nurse in training."

Ruth blushed at all the unexpected praise.

Dr. Wong explained the program in more detail. Ruth would join the Navy Cadet program as a nurse in training, and would attend the accelerated ninety-day nursing program at Linfield College in McMinnville, Oregon. Once she graduated from that program, she would be sworn into the Navy as an Ensign in the US Navy Nurse Corps, and given further training as a surgical nurse in the Navy Hospital in San Diego California. Dr. Wong also emphasized the dire need for nurses, with the war on. "There will be great opportunities for promotion, and you'll learn both Occidental and Oriental medicine, which will be greatly needed for our returning veterans in the coming years."

Everyone had lots of questions about the program. Oscar wanted to know about the pay, and Dr. Wong told him it would be sixty dollars a month for Cadets and one hundred and twenty dollars a month for Ensigns. Oscar nodded, seeming satisfied with the Navy pay, and made no comments about his Norwegian socialism.

Helen wanted to know, if Ruth joined the Navy, when she would have to report for duty. "September 7th," came the answer. Could she come home for Thanksgiving?

"Yes, and maybe Christmas as well."

Ruth had only one question. "I'd be honored to join the program and become an Ensign. Will I get to wear a uniform?"

"Yes," Commander Cash promised. "And you'll travel the world, working as a Navy Nurse, saving the lives of our sailors and soldiers."

It all sounded too good to be true, but that was it. Ruth had found the next chapter in her life! She was ready to volunteer, if Oscar and Helen approved.

"And with her away at nursing school," Dr. Wong said with a sly grin. "The rumors about her exploits will soon die down. It's a win… win for her and the Navy."

Over a delicious meal of beef steaks and potatoes, the conversation continued, the talk ranging from nursing school to the outrageous rumors and, finally, the happenings that could be talked about at fire lookouts. At one point, Ruth remarked to Dr. Wong, "I haven't seen you since my birthday, sir. How was your trip with the pineapple delivery man? Did he get home safely?

"Yes, he's back home in his orange grove with his family," Wong answered. "Did you bring that film he left for me?"

Ruth reached into her purse and gave the canister of film to Dr. Wong. "I bet it was a beautiful reunion."

The doctor nodded. "It was. The last I heard, he was working with the Army to help organize the 442nd Regimental Combat Team of only Nikkei soldiers that will fight in Europe. He's a brave young man with a wonderful family."

"What's a Nikkei?" Oscar asked.

"Just a mutual friend," Ruth told her father.

By the time the evening was over, Ruth and her parents had signed all the necessary papers for Ruth to join the Cadet program. She liked the idea of being in the Navy and living up to the challenges of that Navy Cross. The only person who didn't seem excited about her future was Roy. His girlfriend had just joined the Navy! Their romance would have to take a backseat for the duration of the war.

**Surgical Nurses Graduating Class - May, 1943**

**Pineapples**

The Japanese balloon bombs, or Fu-Go bombs, filled with hydrogen gas started appearing in the Pacific Northwest forests in the early 1940s. These were experimental weapons intended to kill civilians and cause forest fires up and down the West Coast. During the war, Japan launched more than nine thousand such bombs. The balloons, each carrying an anti-personnel bomb and two incendiary bombs, were able to cross the Pacific Ocean in about seventy hours.

The War Department was deeply concerned about these new weapons and sent inspection teams out from Washington, D.C., to study the devices and their mechanisms. As it turned out, all of the bombs had one thing in common: bags of ordinary beach sand was used as ballast. Samples of the sand were sent to Washington, D.C., where geologist studied the origins of the sample.

After months of searching, studying, and heated debates, it was determined which specific Japanese Islands, towns, and personnel were engaged in building and releasing the Fu-Go bombs. The balloons were being made by high school girls scattered around the islands and armed by the military. With this information, the American Government was concerned that the Japanese would also use the balloon delivery system for biological warfare, just as they had done to the Chinese in 1937. That was unacceptable, and in the spring of 1945 the War Department dispatched the Air Force to destroy all the Fu-Go bomb manufacturing and launching sites. The enemy towns were wiped off the map, all because of a few piles of sand and the American scientists back in Washington, D.C.

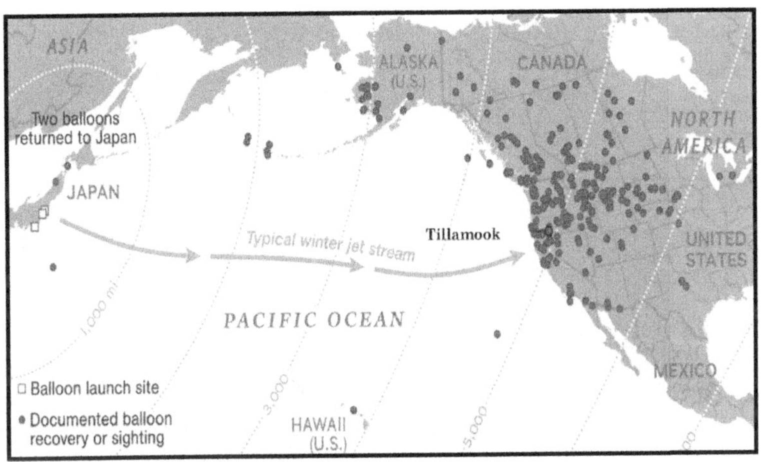


**Fu-Go Recovery and Sightings**

**Submersible Aircraft Carriers**

The I-400-class submarine was a marvelous example of Japanese engineering during WWII. These Imperial boats remained the largest submarines ever built until the construction of nuclear ballistic missile submarines in the 1960s. The Japanese name for this type of submarine was Sentoku. They were submarine aircraft carriers capable of carrying three Aichi M6A aircraft underwater to their destinations. They were designed to surface, launch their planes, then quickly dive again before they were discovered. They also carried torpedoes for close-range combat.

The I-400 class was designed with the range to travel anywhere in the world and return. A fleet of eighteen such boats was planned in 1942, and work started in January of 1943 at the Kure, Hiroshima arsenal. Within a year, however, the plan was scaled back to five boats, of which only three (I-400, and I-401 and I-402) were completed. The mission of these submarines was to attack the Panama Canal and to bomb the forests of the Pacific coast. That mission was never carried out because Japan surrendered on August 15th, 1945.

**I-400 submarine**

### Japanese Internment Camps

Thousands of Japanese Americans, half of whom were children, were incarcerated for up to four years, without due process of law or any factual basis, during WWII. These were remote camps surrounded by barbed wire and armed guards.

Mitsuye Endo was a plaintiff in the landmark Supreme Court lawsuit that ultimately led to the closing of the internment camps in the US and the return of Japanese Americans to the West Coast in 1945.

# Character List

Order of appearance

Ruth Ann Nelson: (Firewatcher)
Winnie: (Ruth's dog)
Nick Nelson: (Ruth's brother)
Helen Nelson: (Ruth's mother)
Oscar Nelson: (Ruth's father)
Herb Wilson: (Owner of Hebo Cafe)
Alice Wilson: (Herb's wife)
Lucy Wilson: (Ruth's friend)
Officer Roy Adams: (Deputy Sheriff)
Mr. Maggot: (Convict)
Sheriff William Adams: (Roy's father)
Mildred Adams: (Roy's mother)
Ellen Adams: (Roy's sister)
Chief Forester Eric Jacobs
Commander Cash
Sam Larson: (County Deputy Sheriff)
Lieutenant JG Wong: (Flight Surgeon)
Dr. Chén Wong: (Lt. JG Wong's father)
Japanese pilot Kai (George) Aoki
Emma Dante Aoki: (George's mother)

**Firewatcher Crew**

Henry Hoyt (*Pops*) Nestucca Dunes
Margaret Smith (*Little Bird*) Crow's Nest
Hank Johnson (*Eagle Eye*) Buzzard Butte
Silver Cloud (*Tonto*) Thunder Mountain
Ruth Nelson (*Cloud Girl*) Hebo Butte

Watch towers came all different sizes, shapes and locations

# Bonus Story

## Christmas Ship 1941

**Santa's Surprise Stop - The SS Mauna Ala**

Christmas can come in all forms and in unexpected ways. So it was for the steamship Mauna Ala on her way to Honolulu Hawaii in early December of 1941.

Departing from Seattle, the 421-foot freighter was hauling a cargo for the US Government, as she was that year's official "Christmas ship." The vessel was packed with 60,000 baled Christmas trees; 10,000 frozen turkeys; 3,000 frozen chickens; and thousands more cases of prime steaks and Almond Roca candy. Her destination, Pearl Harbor, where the soldiers and sailors stationed on the island were eagerly waiting for her arrival.

The sneak attack by the Japanese on December 7, the ***Day of Infamy***, happened when the Mauna Ala was still several thousand miles from her destination. Almost immediately, headquarters in Seattle sent word to terminate the voyage. Pearl Harbor was heavily damaged and clogged with sunken Navy ships. The port was in no condition to host ships that weren't absolutely essential. Plus, a state of war had just broken out, and the Japanese had a world-class submarine fleet. Now was not the time for big, slow and aging steamers like the Mauna Ala to be making unescorted trips across the Pacific. So the ship was ordered to change course for the nearest deep water port. And, unfortunately for the Mauna Ala, that nearest port was Astoria, Oregon.

While the ship was getting turned around, an order was received for total radio silence. Radio transmissions could be triangulated, which meant that the enemy could quickly be able to figure out exactly where to send its submarines to intercept ships using their radios. So as the Mauna Ala steamed homeward, she was neither sending nor receiving any information. And that was unfortunate, because had it not been the case, they surely would have learned that the well-meaning authorities in Oregon had decided to black out the entire coast. And they'd blacked it out completely: including all the lighthouses and the navigational beacons.

Unfortunately the ship's crew did learn these facts eventually. But it was an expensive lesson. The lookouts on the steamer reported the danger roughly an hour after dusk when they saw the ship's running lights gleaming on the top of breakers in the surf just ahead.

And so it was that under full power at maximum cruising speed, the S.S. Mauna Ala piled onto the beach at the Clatsop Spit, just four miles south of the Columbia River Bar with her screws still turning, driving her steel hull deep into the sands and still churning up the waters behind her as she ground shuddering to a stop. When she hit, her officers on the bridge were still actively scanning the horizon looking for the light of the Columbia River Lightship, never realizing that the light had been turned off to keep Japanese marauders from finding their way by it.

The spectacle of a large ship marooned on the Clatsop beach in the dark of night had not gone unnoticed on shore. With rumors flying that the ship was a Japanese landing craft and that the baled Christmas trees were invading soldiers, Warrenton was said to be under attack by Japanese soldiers. Locked and loaded and ready to show the Japanese what a big mistake they'd made, hundreds of volunteer civilians, carrying hunting weapons, converged on the beach, joined by a bunch of other local residents salvaging Christmas trees and cases of steaks out of the surf near the big steamer lying stranded on the beach.

Mindful of what happens to 10,000 turkeys when they're left out in an unrefrigerated space for too long — even in December on the Oregon Coast — the military declared the contents of the Mauna Ala "open salvage," essentially inviting local residents to come on down and get what they could. So, plenty of locals got to start off the nation's four-year wartime run of scarcity and rationing with a whale of a Christmas feast, courtesy of the Mauna Ala and the U.S. military.

*PostScript:* Approximately three thousand ships have met their fate in Oregon waters. The majority of the shipwrecks have occurred on or near the Columbia River Bar, where the ebb tides of the Columbia run into the flood tides of the Pacific. Strong currents, a shallow channel, and powerful winds—which can capsize poorly loaded ships and create foggy conditions—have made the Bar one of the most deadly in the world. Its nickname is the Graveyard of the Pacific.

**One of Many: Remains of the Peter Iredale, October 25, 1906**

## Acknowledgements

During the writing of this book, I am grateful to have had a wonderful team of professionals, friends, and family who helped and supported my efforts.

Judith Myers, my story editor, has collaborated on all my books. She has a magic touch with language and is a joy to work with. Judy knows my writing weaknesses and somehow, like an anchor, she can reel me back into a safe harbor.

And many thanks to Katie Miller who provided a second look at punctuation, and enthusiastic feedback on story development. Her comments and thoughtful observations were invaluable and deeply appreciated.

To my wife of fifty years Tess: who has always been the first to read my stories and provide non-stop encouragement and unwavering support. Her constructive feedback keeps me focused, and her heartfelt enthusiasm keeps me hopeful.

Having said all this, it's my name on the title page, and I am responsible and accountable for every word. Any errors, misinterpretations, or mistakes are solely mine. With that said, I enjoyed writing **Firewatcher** to the last word!

All photographs and graphics used in this book were licensed from museums, came from private collections, were provided by government agencies, were of public domain or found on the internet, all without embedded copyright notices. If I've inadvertently infringed on any copyrights, please give notice and the materials will be removed in forthcoming editions

Brian D. Ratty

## About the Author

**Brian D. Ratty** is a retired media executive, writer, publisher and graduate of Brooks Institute of Photography. He and his wife, Tess, live on the north Oregon Coast, where he writes and photographs that rugged and majestic region. Over the past thirty five years, he has traveled the vast wilderness of the Pacific Coast in search of images and stories that reflect the spirit and splendor of those spectacular lands. Brian is an award-winning author of eleven books and the owner of Sunset Lake Publishing.
**mailto:bdratty@Dutchclarke.com**

## Other Books by Brian Ratty

**More Book Information: Dutchclarke.com**

**Video: How Astoria Oregon Helped Win WWII**

**www.youtube.com/watch?v=Qz93MGFzyUw**

Made in the USA
Middletown, DE
19 December 2022